THE SUMMER I
LOVED YOU

Nicole Bea

A NineStar Press Publication

www.ninestarpress.com

The Summer I Loved You

Printed in the USA

ISBN: 978-1-64890-348-9

First Edition, August, 2021

Also available in eBook, ISBN: 978-1-64890-347-2

CONTENT WARNING:
This book contains sexual content, which may only be suitable for mature readers. Depictions of cheating and references to a dead parent.

To warm nights, the universal language of music, and kisses under the stars. May the most enchanted summers stay with you always.

Shy pianist Shae is looking forward to a summer of fun in her small hometown before she leaves to study music at the University of Tampa, Florida. After saying goodbye to her mother–who is leaving to visit her Canadian rodeo-clown boyfriend for six weeks–Shae meets up with her boyfriend Evan and her best friend Livi to organize plans, but is quickly thrown for a loop when they announce they have been cheating together.

As Shae's perfect summer quickly turns into a perfect disaster, she has a run-in with traveling guitarist Asher Lohan who is in town just for a single week. Unable to resist their sudden attraction, opposite personalities, and reeling with residual pain from their pasts, Shae and Asher soon find themselves falling into a summer that is punctuated with broken friendships, self-discovery, and learning to trust again.

Chapter One

SHAE

Most things in my life can be compared to music. There seems to be a piece for everything I've ever experienced, a symphony or sonata that perfectly captures my emotional state at any given moment in time. Like when Luke Bartholemew suddenly decided to kiss me at recess in front of the whole seventh grade class. I was just standing there watching Jake Turner pound Liz Whalen with a dodgeball and then, *smack*! There were Luke's lips. I got the same feeling once when I was listening to the second movement of Haydn's *Surprise* symphony with headphones on and the volume was way too loud. It was jarring and uncomfortable and about as fun as being hit with a dodgeball.

Or like when my mom and dad finalized their divorce. I was going through an Elgar phase at the time, and somehow, I found myself comforted by the grandness and melancholy of the "Nimrod" theme in his *Enigma Variations*. My own feelings were kind of an enigma to me, a mixture of sadness and growing awareness that my parents were as fallible as anyone else, and it was freeing to feel those same emotions reverberating through an orchestral string section.

But my real passion has always been for classical piano. I think it's the way the keys respond to even the lightest touch. The emotions are mine to interpret, mine to make echo through the house or hall and touch someone else's soul, recalling memories of their own. Even when I'm terrified onstage, the moment my fingers find the keys, it's like the rest of the world disappears.

Today I'm practicing Debussy, his *Reflets dans l'eau* that I've been trying to memorize for the better part of three weeks. The window of the living room is open to let in the morning breeze and sound of waves crashing along the beach, a perfect counterpoint to the flowing lines that make Debussy so popular.

I can already tell the day is going to be gorgeous. Maybe it's the music, or the smell of salt air wafting through the aged glass panes, but my mind isn't really on the fingering I'm trying to perfect. It's wandering over the sand, feeling ripples of water lap against my bare toes, enjoying the bright sunshine of a perfect summer day in Florida. In my mind, there's even a crab scuttling along the sand nearby, droplets of ocean water dazzling on its back. Just as I'm about to move my hand so I don't get pinched, my finger slips from B flat to B natural by mistake. I wince and stop playing.

"Sounds pretty." Mom clasps on an earring as she rushes around the open concept living and dining area, her two suitcases in the entryway of our old house. By the way she's running about, she's already late for her flight, but she keeps distracting herself with popping in on me.

Mom's obviously nervous about leaving me here in Emerald Beach by myself for six weeks, as nervous as she is about seeing her long-distance boyfriend Will for the first time in half a year. He's a Floridian but lives in Canada now, somewhere in the western part where he works as a rodeo clown. I wish I were making that up, but I'm not. Mom's dating life is basically a theme and variations in the worst possible way. Every six months or so, she finds herself a new version of the same insecure guy, and each one is quirkier or weirder or more dramatic than the next.

"It sounds like garbage," I sigh under my breath, but Mom doesn't hear me because she's run back to the hall to shove something else in her suitcase. I toss a strand of my long, dark hair behind my shoulder, my skin already feeling sticky as the temperature creeps up with the sun, and stare out of the window at one of the palms that hangs over the sidewalk. The Debussy is on the list of pieces I'm supposed to be preparing for my new studio teacher when fall semester starts. It's only the University of Tampa, but their music performance program is still competitive, and I know I need to show up ready to prove I belong.

You can have a Frozen Rocket if you can play the quasi cadenza passage twenty times with no mistakes. It's an old trick, promising myself rewards for practicing. Hopefully, it will help me work through my distraction so I can move on to the rest of my pieces. Maybe by the time I'm done practicing, Evan will be able to slip away from his family's ice cream shop and grab an early lunch.

I set my fingers on the keys and two things happen at once: Mom comes back into the room, stomping into her espadrilles and carrying a sweater she definitely won't need until she gets to Canada, and my phone dings with a text.

Mom speaks before I can read what the message says. "You sure you're going to be okay here by yourself for most of the summer? I mean, this is a big responsibility, Shaeline. I'm trusting you with a lot."

She only calls me by my full name when something serious is happening. "Everything will be fine. I'll be working and going to the beach with Evan and Livi. Plus, I need to practice." I gesture toward the piano. "There's something about this piece I can't get right."

Mom nods the way she does when she's trying to reassure herself and pulls her phone absently from her pocket, looking down at the screen. "I've got to go, the taxi's here." She lifts her head to fix me with her most mom-like stare. "Listen, no parties, okay? You have the car if you need it but remember to keep it full of gas, and don't leave the city. Be responsible, please."

I make an *X* over my heart as my phone dings again, reminding me of my own unread message. "I promise. Besides, I'm almost nineteen, Mom. I can take care of myself for a few weeks. Go have a nice time."

She looks at me wistfully for a moment before kicking herself into high gear, kissing the top of my head and grabbing her suitcases.

"Okay. I've got my passport, my wallet, my phone, my charger..." Mom starts ticking things off out loud as the taxi horn beeps to remind her that it's still there waiting. "Oop! All right, Shae. Be good. I'll call you when I arrive at Will's. His address and phone number are on the fridge."

"Bye, Mom. Have a good summer."

"You too!" She calls to me as the screen door slams shut.

I sit there on the piano bench listening to the sound of the taxi backing out of our driveway, and then our little beachside street is quiet with the harmony of the waves and the chirrup of birds. The serenity is shattered by another ding from my phone, and I finally pick it up to read.

EVAN: *Wanna meet for breakfast?*

SHAE: *Sure. Barracuda's? I desperately need a Frozen Rocket.*

EVAN: *Hitting the sugar syrup a little early today, huh?*

SHAE: *Always.*

EVAN: *:) See you in ten.*

Evan's ten minutes really means twenty when he's at the shop, which also means I can squeeze in my twenty repetitions to "earn" my frozen treat if I concentrate. Inhaling a deep breath of salty ocean air, I adjust myself on the piano bench and hover my hands over the keys with my eyes closed, like I always do before starting a piece. It grounds me in the music to come and helps me focus. Especially on days like today when the beach is calling to me. I'll be out there soon enough, tossing back icy drinks with my boyfriend and making plans for how to spend the next six weeks of summer. *Beach bonfires, volleyball, paddle boarding...trying to convince Livi to swim more and tan less.* That last thought makes me smirk. Best friends don't always have to share the same interests, but Livi never seems to understand that you can get just as tan from playing at the beach as you can from lying on it.

I lower my fingers and begin to play. The first page flows by and then I'm into the quasi cadenza. One repetition, fine. Two repetitions, still fine. Three repetitions, and I fumble the fingering and have to start over. Thinking about my summer plans instead of visualizing the piece's score wasn't very helpful. I fix the score in my mind and pretend each of the notes is a tiny little Frozen Rocket.

Fifteen minutes later, I leave the corner of Mermaid Avenue and make my way across Emerald Beach's lazy main street toward the row of shops and restaurants that borders the waterfront. My dark hair hangs in waves around my shoulders, and the gentle breeze off the water is blowing the smell of sea salt and tea tree shampoo into my face. It's a familiar aroma—Evan's favorite—a scent of long days spent stuck in school longing for the beach and warm nights spent on the sand with friends around the bonfire.

Barracuda's is on the far end of the street, right where Main intersects with Emerald Drive. It's my favorite restaurant in town, and not just because they serve the best frozen drinks. The back wall of the dining room has a great view down the beach to the water and there is a large deck with umbrella-covered booth seating for those who prefer ocean breezes to ceiling fans. The interior is decorated like a cross between a fishing boat and a beach hut.

I push open the door and scan the interior, looking for Evan. There are several tables full of customers, locals and tourists alike eating their way through heaps of fluffy scrambled eggs and stacks of macadamia nut pancakes drizzled with coconut syrup. A group near the front windows catches my eye, its occupants waving as they notice my arrival.

"Hey, Shae!" they call in scattered chorus. Marley and Jessica are there, both former members of our high school orchestra, along with their boyfriends Derek and Mark and a couple of other guys from the old football team. Evan played on the team, too, before we all graduated.

"Come join us!" Marley says excitedly. "I finally got my letter from Northwestern and I got the full-ride scholarship I applied for! We're celebrating!" Beside her, Derek is wolfing his way through his food. He looks up and gives me a friendly smile.

I return it, but it doesn't come automatically because I've been put on the spot with all the sudden attention, and the old nervousness is creeping into my stomach. They don't mean to make me uncomfortable; it always happens this way.

"Maybe later. I'm meeting Evan for breakfast."

A tall girl in a bright-yellow polo comes out from the kitchen carrying a tray of full plates.

"Morning, Shae!"

"Morning, Tali. Have you seen Evan?"

She nods her head, dark ponytail swishing, toward the back doors. "He's out on the deck. Just brought out his coffee. Should I bring you the usual?"

"Yes please." I nod my thanks to Tali and make my way out to the back deck, thinking about how amazing a Frozen Rocket is going to taste after practicing all morning. I'm probably the only person who even orders the kid's drink since it's been taken off the menu, but I can't help myself. The blue raspberry slush at the bottom is so good—like stepping in the coolness of the ocean after a hot day spent indoors with broken air conditioning.

As I slip my way through the late morning crowds toward the outdoor portion of the restaurant, I quickly spot Evan sitting in one of the rattan booth seats. His brown hair looks rumpled like he's run his hand through it too many times after getting out of the gulf water, which wouldn't surprise me considering the heat wave Florida's been having.

"Hey, sorry I'm late." I set my phone down on the table and slide into the seat across from him. "Had to get a little more practice in before I came, and I thought your mom would keep you longer in the shop."

"It's fine. I don't have to be in the shop for a bit anyway. Has your mom left yet?" Evan's voice is light as he lifts his coffee mug for a sip.

"Yeah, she left about twenty minutes ago. I'm on my own for the next six weeks. Time to start talking about plans." I put out a hand to Evan, the usual sign we use for holding hands with each other. His fingers wrap around mine and he gently pulls me closer to lean across the table. There's a mischievous glint in his eye that I recognize from our nights making out on the beach under the pier.

"So, I've been thinking about how you're going away to Tampa in the fall. What that means for us, you know? We haven't really talked about it."

I roll my eyes in mock irritation. "Right, because Tampa is *so* far away and we've only been dating for three years. How could we possibly stand the separation?"

The corner of Evan's mouth twitches with a smile, but instead of laughing he tightens his grip on my hand. "I'm serious, Shae. What if you get up there and you meet some piano guy who starts hitting on you?"

"Have you seen the guys who are into classical music around here? There's a reason all the orchestra girls are dating guys on the football team, me included." I give him a little slap on the back of the hand like I'm hitting a staccato chord on the piano. "You've got nothing to worry about."

"I just want to know you aren't going to leave and forget about me, you know?" His brow furrows with concern. "To know that what we have is special."

It hadn't occurred to me to think Evan would be worried about the potential fragility of our relationship. "What are you getting at?"

He shrugs, but I can tell he actually does have a point in mind. "I just thought it might be nice if we did something to show each other that we're for real. And, you know, now that your mom is gone and you've got the house to yourself, it might be time to take our relationship to the—"

"There you are!" An irritated voice cuts over Evan as Livi, my best friend, stomps her way up from the beach onto the restaurant deck, a mesh beach bag swinging from one shoulder and a pair of Kate Spade sunglasses hiding her green eyes from view. She's tall and curvy in all the ways I'm not, like the photo original to my negative, and her tanned skin glows against the white of her sun dress.

Evan yanks his hand out of mine and seizes his coffee cup again. He takes a deliberate swig.

"I thought you were going to wait for me outside the shop," Livi says in a pouty tone. Then her posture grows stiff, as though she's realized something unpleasant. It's hard to tell what she's looking at because of the sunglasses, but that on-the-spot churning feeling is in my stomach again and I'm not entirely convinced it's only because my boyfriend was hinting that we should—well, *you know*—for the first time.

"Uh, no, I uh..." Evan is stammering and looking uncomfortable. He stares between the two of us in confusion until Livi heaves a dramatic sigh and perches herself on the end of his booth bench.

"Morning, Shae," she says, but her voice is frosty rather than its usual friendly. "I didn't realize you were going to be here." She takes off her sunglasses and puts them on the table, her hand brushing against Evan's where it sits still clamped around his coffee mug.

I resist the urge to let my jaw drop in surprise. Why on earth wouldn't I be here, having breakfast with my boyfriend? And why on earth would my best friend, of all people, not expect that? "Well, I guess I am." It's *such* a lame response, but it's already out of my mouth.

Livi leans against Evan's shoulder and I swear I see her glance toward the interior of the restaurant to see how many other people are nearby. It's not unusual for Evan and Livi to sit next to each other—it happens all the time—but there's something about the *way* she leans against him, and how he instinctively tilts his head toward hers that gives me a strange tingling feeling along the back of my neck.

"Is everything...okay?"

"Of course," Evan says automatically, but the response is too quick. "I just...uh...well, there's been a change in my...plans for the summer. That's what I wanted to...to talk about."

My stomach drops. "What do you mean, a change in plans?" I glance toward Livi, but she's purposefully turned toward the restaurant now, her blonde curls blowing in the wind and her green eyes everywhere but meeting my own.

Tali appears just then to drop off my Frozen Rocket. "You guys ready to order?" she asks.

Evan avoids my gaze and instead looks toward Livi, who kicks him under the table. "I think we need another minute."

That gets Tali's attention. We're regulars, we know the menu by heart and should be able to order breakfast without a second thought. She looks between the three of us with a frown. "Uh, sure, just wave me down when you're ready." Her brown eyes settle on me for a moment longer than the others. Something is *definitely* up if Tali is giving me her suspicious look.

She walks away, and I catch a glimpse of Marley and the others at their table on the other side of the restaurant. The guys are still joking and eating, but Jessica is whispering to Marley and both are watching our table with curious expressions.

There's an awkward silence, and I realize suddenly that I've left my empty hand on the table all this time. I withdraw it and try to pick up the threads of the conversation. "So...what were you saying about a change of plans?"

A new look comes into Evan's eyes, a decidedly guilty one. "It's not exactly my plans, I mean, sort of, but it's more like—"

"Oh, for God's sake," Livi interrupts with a shake of her blonde curls. "Evan's breaking up with you, Shae."

My head suddenly feels like a jumbled mess—like John Cage's frenetic *Music of Changes* is blasting full-bore in my brain—and I lean against the woven back of the bench, staring hard at both of them. "Excuse me?"

"I think you heard me. Evan doesn't want to be with you anymore."

Chapter Two

SHAE

The expression on my face must be terrible because Evan leans forward and tries to reach for me again. "Look, it's not as bad as it sounds. We're going to Europe, so we won't even be around."

My mouth is dry, so I swallow and force myself to speak. "Really? Because it sounds pretty bad to me. And Europe? Really?" My voice is croaky and hoarse, like I've been yelling at the top of my lungs. *This can't possibly be true. Wasn't he just telling me he wanted*—that stops my train of thought dead in its tracks and my cheeks suddenly feel like they're on fire. It's all too disjointed, none of it fits together. Why would he talk about *that* if he was going to break up with me? Somewhere there's a piece that I'm missing, a sharp I forgot to add while changing keys, *something* that my dazed mind can't—or won't—process.

And then the key change resolves and I realize the truth.

"You're breaking up with me for Livi." Hot tears prickle at the corners of my eyes but I can't tell if they're hurt tears or angry tears—or both. I don't want either of them to see me cry if this is the truth, because I feel like I should at least be strong for my own dignity's sake until I can go hide in my bedroom and punch my pillow. My heart, on the other hand, could give a Picardy third about dignity; it could probably explode out of my chest at any second, breaking through my ribs.

Evan nods, but Livi doesn't react at all. She's frozen there, like a best friend popsicle, icier than my forgotten and rapidly melting Frozen Rocket.

"How long?"

Evan's face goes slack. "What do you mean?"

"How long have you been planning this?"

Again, Livi kicks Evan under the table. "Maybe a week. I don't know. I thought that I could keep it a secret from each of you." He hesitates just enough that I'm instantly sure it's a lie. "I'm sorry, Shae," he adds quickly, "I just—"

"Don't! I don't want to hear excuses!" The words cut out from my mouth so sharp I swear my lips must be bleeding, but instead of letting Evan try to placate me again, I grab my phone and slide out of the booth. I'm turned around and heading out of the door of Barracuda's when a tear slips from my eye, and I practically smash my hand against my cheek to rub it away so it doesn't leave a red streak on my skin.

"Shae!" Evan calls after me, but I don't turn around. Instead, I crash through the front entryway of the restaurant, not even giving Tali or Marley or anyone a chance to ask what's wrong. It feels like everyone in the restaurant is staring at me and I'm hit with an impulse to turn around and flip off Evan and curse them both out while leaving with my head held high, followed immediately by an over-whelming urge to throw up.

Instead, I hide around the corner of the building, un-lock my phone, and delete his and Livi's information from my contacts list.

There. Now they're gone forever, and I don't have to think about them anymore.

As if.

My brain has gone into major panic mode, the same feeling I get with my stage fright, but on steroids. All I can think of is getting home. Getting home and locking the door against any half-hearted attempt by Evan to apolo-gize, or by Marley and Jessica to ask what happened. Then I laugh out loud to myself. Evan, at least, won't come. He's probably got Livi wrapped around him in that booth right now, happy to forget about me and my abandoned Frozen Rocket. I feel a pang of sadness for the loss of my icy sugar, but it can't be helped now. I just need to get myself home, and then I can play out my sorrows on the piano and watch trashy television while drinking sweet tea. I deserve it.

Wiping another tear from the corner of my eye, I don't even bother to check for traffic as I dart into Main Street. Everyone jaywalks here, and drivers know to slow down and watch for pedestrians. I'm halfway across when suddenly the air splits with the sound of a blaring car ste-reo and a minivan that appears to be polka-dotted comes careening around the corner. The driver and I see each other at the same moment. His eyes widen and he slams his foot on the brake, but he's not quick enough. The van slides on the loose gravel and sand that always dust the road surface, the driver tugging hard on the wheel to swerve around me.

I try to dart out of the way, but my foot catches on a crack in the road and I go down close to the curb, noticing belatedly that the van has a dent in the front bumper. It's an odd thing to notice when I'm about to be run down by a bunch of vacationing frat boys blasting scratchy rock music from their stereo moments after finding out that my best friend and boyfriend have been cheating on me together. What a classic Florida headline that will make when my death shows up in the evening news.

I'm not dead, obviously, but I'm definitely shaken. There's a good-sized scrape on my knee and my hands are stinging. The van is stopped now and the door slides back at the same moment I realize the vehicle isn't polka-dotted at all but has band stickers pasted on the passenger's side doors: Red Hot Chili Peppers, AC/DC, A Perfect Circle, Flogging Molly, and others with logos I don't know or can't read at this angle. The open door reveals three occupants in the van, all staring at me. Of course, right at that moment, a sob gets stuck in my throat and I make a weird hiccupping noise over the idling engine.

"Hey!" the passenger shouts, not bothering to turn the music down as he yells through the window at me. His blond hair hangs in curls around his face. "Are you out of your mind? You can't just run through the road like—"

A raven-haired boy in the back seat punches the passenger in the arm and then scrambles out of the open side door. My overwrought mind catches details about him too: the tattoo of flowers running down his arm and the bootcut jeans that are way too heavy for the temperature outside but that emphasize his thighs so much it's nearly worth the fact he's probably sweating to death.

He jogs up to me. "Are you okay?"

I nod, the twisting feeling in my stomach only increasing as I stare into the clearest pool-blue eyes I've ever seen in my life. "I-I think so." The words come out as a stammer, and suddenly tears are threatening to fall again.

"Hey, it's okay," the boy says, reaching out a hand in a comforting sort of way, and before I can process the gesture, I've already accepted his help and am back on my feet. He doesn't let go right away, as though he's worried I'm going to lose my balance and fall over again. "Sorry about Gabe's driving. I told him to slow down."

"It's not that." My stomach feels like it's wobbling up and down like when my family vacationed in the mountains one time when I was in sixth grade and we took a long, winding road.

The boy gives me a nod of understanding and then seems to suddenly remember that we're holding hands. He lets go and instead stuffs his hands into his pockets, eyes zipping down and catching sight of the bleeding scrape on my knee. "Ouch! That doesn't look good." He looks around at his friends, one of whom has climbed onto his seat and is lounging in the middle of the van's skylight, looking annoyed.

"Asher! Let's go!" the driver shouts with a punctuating honk of the van's horn.

"Ask her where the beach parking is!" his other friend calls from the skylight.

"In a minute!" The boy—Asher—yells back, and then gives me a regretful look. "I don't think we have a first aid kit in the van or anything, but maybe we can give you a lift?"

There's a sudden glint of light from the door of Barracuda's across the street that sends me back into panic mode. Someone probably heard the tire squeal when the van slammed on its brakes and is coming out to investigate. The last thing I want is for the whole restaurant to swarm out and see the state I'm in after being dumped and almost run over.

I need to get out of here! "I'm fine. I only live down the road a bit this way." I give a frantic sort of wave in the direction of Mermaid Avenue and words keep tumbling out of my mouth. "Um, the beach access is all pedestrian. Probably another couple miles in the direction of the water. Best bet is to park out front of Barracuda's just on the right, go inside, get a drink, and then go out through the back. I recommend a Frozen Rocket and that you tell my ex-boyfriend he's a complete ass for cheating on me with my best friend!"

And I turn on my heel and take off down the sidewalk just as a figure steps into the sunlight in front of Barracuda's. Asher shouts after me, telling me to wait, but the panic pushes me forward and dulls the ache of my scraped knee and hands until I fumble my way through the front door of my house on Mermaid Avenue.

Chapter Three

ASHER

It takes me about two seconds after walking into Barracuda's to spot the couple out on the back deck in a rattan-covered booth. They look way too cozy sitting next to each other, and there's an empty seat across from them with an abandoned drink dripping red and blue liquid onto the tabletop. I know instinctively that they're the people the girl from the street was talking about, and I can't help picturing her sitting there while the guy says he's been cheating on her with the curly-haired blonde next to him.

Music is pumping from a hidden speaker somewhere, playing that new Charlie Puth hit—the one about wishing for your ex to be cheated on. It's ironically appropriate. There's a debate going on in my head, the angry part of me wanting to stomp over and say something to them, but the smarter half wins out. I stay the hell quiet and follow my bandmates Gabe and Chance to a table on the opposite side of the deck, out in the sun.

"So, what's the plan for the week, then?" Gabe pulls out a chair and plunks down on the stained wood just as a server comes over: dark-skinned, ponytail, curvy.

"What can I get you guys?" She sounds casual, but her eyes are hard as they dart a glance at the couple in the other booth. It's a good bet she knows the couple and the girl Gabe nearly ran over; she probably saw everything when those two lovesick puppies broke that poor girl's heart.

"Coffee, black." Gabe gives the girl a smile. "Might as well bring two cups of it."

Chance flips through a tabletop menu like he's going to order a drink even though he's still underage. "I'll just take a water and a root beer."

Ponytail looks over at me, waiting for my order, and I remember what the girl in the street said about a drink. "Can I get a Frozen Rocket?"

The hard look in her eyes suddenly intensifies. "You're not the ones who almost ran Shae over, are you?"

"Hey, it wasn't our fault! She just darted out into the middle of the road like a maniac!" Chance exclaims.

"It was an accident," Gabe says and throws out a restraining hand to his cousin. "But we stopped and made sure she was okay, didn't we, Ash?"

The server—Tali, as per her name tag—is glaring at me again, so I nod quickly. "I got out and checked on her. She had a scraped knee and some scratches on her hands, but she said she didn't want help. Told me to order a Frozen Rocket and then took off down the street. I think she was upset about—something." I leave out the part about calling the guy in the other booth an ass.

Some of the heat drains from Tali's attitude. "You're right about that." She throws another dirty look at the couple, who now have their lips locked together, and then shakes her ponytail back and forth. "So, you want a Frozen Rocket, huh? It hasn't been on the menu for a year. Shae's the only one who ever remembers to order it now."

I feel the guys' eyes on me, silently questioning my next move.

"Should I even ask what it is at this point?"

Tali laughs, and I marvel at the speed of her emotional one-eighty. The lovebirds in the booth unstick themselves from each other for a moment and glance in our direction to see what's so funny.

"Lemonade, blue food coloring, some cherry flavoring, crushed ice...you'll like it. It's meant for kids, sure, but you'll like it."

Chance snorts. "Asher practically *is* a kid. At heart I mean. Not in the—"

Gabe kicks him under the table; he's always covering up for Chance's big mouth.

Tali forces an uncomfortable smile, like we're the lamest group of customers to have ever graced her presence. "I'll be back."

I watch her turn the corner to the serving station and bar, then look back to find Gabe and Chance both staring at me across the table.

"What?"

"A Frozen Rocket? Who are you?" Chance smirks, running a hand over his jaw. "That girl did a number on you, didn't she?"

"Who, Shae?" I reply, leaning back in my chair, the breeze off the water rustling my hair. The sound of her name makes my heart do a little flip in my chest. We only talked for a moment, but somehow, I can tell the name suits her. It's odd to learn the name of a girl like that, from a stranger instead of in her own voice. And sure, maybe I had a *bit* of an attraction to her, standing there on the side of the road, but it was just a random brush with a stranger. I know what Chance would see it as—hell, what Gabe would see it as, too, under the right circumstances. They would take a meeting like that as an opening, but unlike them, I don't crave one-night stands and random hookups with girls we meet on the road. I want...*more.*

They're still waiting for a response, so I shrug as casually as I can manage. "Just thought I'd take a drink order from a local, is all. She probably knows the best stuff in the area."

Chance and Gabe exchange glances, and I know they don't believe me, but they know better than to say anything more.

"So, you were asking for a plan?" I cough out the words, trying my hardest to change the subject. "I was thinking we'd just laze around on the beach and eat and, you know, do whatever. It's only a week until we have to head to Tampa for the Buskers Festival. We might as well do our relaxing now."

Gabe nods, tapping his fingertips on the table like he's playing his keyboard. "Relaxing. Hmmm. I could get behind that."

Tali returns with our drink order just then, silently setting all the cups in front of us before she heads back off across the restaurant again, pulls a bill from her apron, and hands it to the lovebirds in the corner. As Gabe and Chance talk about what songs we should play in what order at the festival, I take an absent sip of my Frozen

Rocket and allow my mind to wander. The lemonade is tart against whatever flavor the blue section of the layered drink is, and the red has a little bit of sweetness. Altogether, it's pretty good, and somehow reminds me of Shae standing there on the road under the sign that said Mermaid Avenue. Her dark hair was in waves around her shoulders like some kind of ocean goddess, the crystal of her eyes only dulled a little by the tears she was trying so desperately to hide.

As I think about her, my heart starts to race again, though it could be all the sugar in the drink.

"Asher, do you think we should start with 'Broken Glass' or 'Love Letters in the Sand'?" Chance's voice brings me back down to earth, and I realize I'm slurping at the bottom of the Frozen Rocket.

"What?" I reply instinctively, even though I half heard the question. "Probably 'Broken Glass.' I think it'll draw in a crowd right away."

Gabe smirks, leaning back in his chair to take a sip of his steaming black coffee. "I told you he'd say that."

Chance just rolls his eyes, poking his straw in and out of the melting ice in the bottom of his root beer. He doesn't like when he doesn't get his way, and he also doesn't like being wrong. Especially when it comes to my opinion; whatever I think, he usually takes the opposite side.

We finish the dregs of our drinks in the quiet of the salty air, and I twist around to watch people walk along the shoreline, kicking their feet at the water's edge. The lovebirds finally get up and leave after a while, a hushed conversation with barely hidden smiles on their lips as though they still need to keep what they're doing a secret.

And as I watch everyone in their shorts, bare feet, and swimsuits, I start to think up the lyrics to a song in my head and I wish I had a way to write them down. Instead, I repeat the words over and over again so hopefully they're memorized by the time we get back to our rental condo and I have my notebook.

After leaving Barracuda's through the back exit, the guys and I walk along Emerald Beach for what feels like forever. The shore just goes on and on and on until our legs are tired and we're hungry and have to turn around and head back. We talk about our band and music, and Chance and Gabe talk about girls and what life might be like if and when we "make it," while I think. Think about the song I started writing in the restaurant and think about Shae and those sad eyes I want to make happy again somehow.

It's later at night when I finally have an opportunity to sit down with my guitar, long after Chance and Gabe have retreated to their respective bedrooms that they claimed earlier in the day. The third room, the smallest but with the best view and a small bathroom, is mine; it overlooks the lights of Emerald Beach and in the distance, I can see the waves breaking over the sandy shoreline. Headlights from cars pass below me, the full-length windows showing everything the Beach has to offer.

I crawl on top of the covers of the bed with my notebook, and scribble down the lyrics that have been rolling around in my brain.

> *The eyes are crystals; the air's nothing but a breeze*
>
> *I'm in the passenger's seat and someone else has the keys*

The blue's in front of us with the dark gray behind

I'm tangled and twisted up and my soul's so un-kind

But she's there and she's barely breathing

I'm here and my heart is bleeding

And I push through the three-in-the-morning thoughts

And I push through all the three-in-the-morning thoughts

As we turn off

And we turn on

Around the corner of a little place

Called Mermaid Avenue

Humming the words through a couple of times, I strum a chord or two to try to get the rhythm of the words down just right. Normally, after a few passes through the song I'd start fitting in Gabe and Chance's instrumentals as well, working the notes for Gabe's deeper voice. However, with this song, there's something more personal about it, like it's meant to just be played and sung by one person in an acoustic performance in some small coffee shop in the dark and smoke and shadows.

But she's there and she's barely breathing

I'm here and my heart is bleeding

And I push through the three-in-the-morning thoughts...

My phone blinks on the corner of the queen-sized mattress, jingling with an email that's probably spam. It forces me to look at the screen, though, and I see that it is, in fact, three in the morning. The moon is hanging low over the gulf, rippling a milky white across the indigo surface of the water, and there's something beautiful and serene about the whole scene. I tuck my guitar back in the case, pull off my shirt and shorts, and crawl underneath the crisp sheets to watch the world go by and think through those three-in-the-morning thoughts.

★

I must be more tired than I think I am because I wake up hours later to the smell of bacon wafting underneath my bedroom door. Late morning sunlight is streaming through the windows, hitting the glass indirectly and making shapes along the hardwood floor, caressing the case of my guitar and my haphazardly thrown clothes and suitcase. I'm just about to roll out of the covers when there's a knock on the door.

"Asher? You want bacon?" Gabe's voice trickles through. Of course, he's the one up and acting like an adult. He's only a year older than Chance and me, but he acts as if he's our dad sometimes.

"Yeah," I call, easing my way off the mattress and rubbing my tattoo sleeve. "Gimme a minute."

Footsteps retreat as I pull on a pair of shorts from the pile of clothes on the back of a chair and run a hand through my hair in front of the full-length mirror on the closet door. A couple of pieces won't sit straight, but I'm going to shower anyway, and I can guarantee the other guys don't look any better than this, so I walk out into the blasting air conditioning of the main living space.

"You were up late," Chance comments, sitting at the kitchen bar and stuffing his mouth full of crispy bacon strips. We bought three packages, along with some other essentials, at the supermarket when we arrived in town, but I think Gabe's cooking up all of the bacon right now.

I take a seat next to Chance, pulling out a stool and hopping up on the cushion.

"Had a—" I'm about to say that I had a song to write, but something inside me doesn't want to share what I wrote just yet. "Had a song stuck in my head. Wanted to figure out the chords on the guitar. Ever just have something on your mind and it won't go away? Something like that."

Chance nods, and Gabe flips a pile of bacon onto a green plate and hands it over to me. "Something like that, huh? I don't hear you sing very often. But you were singing last night."

"Like I said." I chomp down on a hot strip, burning my tongue in the process. "Song in my head."

"Girl in your head, more like it." Chance teases, and Gabe just smiles with a dumb highlighter-yellow spatula in his hand, standing the utensil up straight.

I shake my head, the lie probably palpable. "No girl, just music. Like always."

"Like always," Gabe repeats, turning back to the stove.

Chance picks up another piece of bacon and crunches it, looking back to where his phone is propped up against a banana and scrolling through photos on what I assume is one of the band's social media accounts.

"Anything good?" I ask, taking a more careful second bite of breakfast. "Pictures from the last show?"

"More like pictures from after the last show." Chance waggles his eyebrows at me, and I punch him in the shoulder. Grinning, he flicks off the screen of his phone and flips it upside down so I can't sneak a peek at whatever he was actually looking at.

"Dude, you're gross. I don't know what those girls see in you."

"It's not about what they see in me, it's about what they—"

"Okay," Gabe cuts in, flicking off the oven and slapping his spatula against the empty frying pan. "We're eating here. Let's just try to have a nice day without getting on one another's nerves, all right?"

"If you ask us what the plan is today, Gabe, I swear to—" Chance slings together a slew of curse words. "Just don't do it." It's a lame ending after all the expletives.

"Fine, no plans. But for your information, I'm going to be at the beach. Probably check out that ice cream parlor we passed on the boardwalk yesterday, places like that always have weird local flavors. Generally just enjoy myself and pretend I don't have to babysit my idiot cousin for a whole day. Asher's allowed to come though." Gabe has a little, joking twinkle in his eye as he steals a piece of bacon from Chance's nearly empty plate and sticks it in his mouth before Chance can protest.

The suggestion actually doesn't sound half bad, but what I really want to do is spend some more time working on that song. My thoughts are already wandering back to it, trying to determine the second verse, what the bridge should be about, but I won't really figure it out until I've got my guitar back in my hands.

"I'm gonna shower," I say, more because I feel like it's rude to just stand up and leave. "Maybe I'll catch up with you at that ice cream place?"

"I got dibs!" Chance yells, scrambling out of his chair and off toward the main bathroom, forgetting my room has a small one of its own and there's no need to race for it.

Gabe rolls his eyes and picks up Chance's abandoned plate. "Loser." He sets the plate in the sink and then picks up the frying pan and starts dumping the congealing grease into the garbage can. "So, you up for coming with me or what?"

I shrug. "Maybe. I want to practice a bit too."

"I thought taking a relaxing week off was your idea."

He's got me there. "It was, but I just…want to play for a bit."

The frying pan clatters into the sink with the other dishes and Gabe rests his hands on either side of the metal basin, giving me the look he only gets when he's about to say something serious. "It's that girl, isn't it? You were up last night writing a song about her."

I shove a piece of bacon into my mouth instead of replying.

"Come on, man. You can't pretend you aren't interested in this kind of stuff. I was there when you were with Sasha. Yeah, she was a piece of work, but whatever. You were totally into her and she was into you, and it never made sense why you broke things off."

Sasha... He just had to go and bring up the girl who claimed she was in love with me until I told her I wasn't ready to let our relationship get physical too fast. She didn't even bother dumping me before she found someone else to screw around with. She never even gave me a chance to explain *why* I wanted to wait. The answer was that we hadn't been together long enough, that I needed something...*more* out of a relationship before I could be ready. I don't know exactly what *more* is in this context, but we definitely didn't have it.

But that's not how Gabe thinks. He won't understand if I try to explain it, so I just shrug again and keep stuffing my mouth with bacon until his shoulders droop in exasperation.

"One of these days, dude, I'm gonna get you to open up. Until then, just remember that it's okay to have a little fun every once in a while, all right? I won't force you to come now, but I expect to see you at that Beaches N' Cream place at noon to eat your way through Beachcomber's Horde or whatever stupid names they've given to their flavors." He points at me to emphasize his words and then leaves the kitchen.

I escape back into my bedroom, humming the lyrics in my head. It's just the moment I close the door that I think up what's supposed to come next, so I grab my notebook and a pen and scribble down the next verse and a repeated chorus.

> *I wake in the empty morning, the space next to me cold*

I'm barely awake and I'm chaos and uncontrolled

The sunrise is lemonade; but life's nothing but a fray

My heart's beating but it's distant and astray

The ocean's in front of us with the sandy edge of white

I'm indigo and she's all the stars in the night

But she's there and she's barely breathing

I'm here and my heart is bleeding

And I push through the three-in-the-morning thoughts

And I push through all the three-in-the-morning thoughts

As we turn off

And we turn on

Around the corner of a little place

Called Mermaid Avenue

Chapter Four

SHAE

I wake up much too early. The sunrise is the color of cotton candy, light blues and bright pinks all mixed together amid the sky. Faint music is coming from somewhere underneath me, and I realize I fell asleep before turning off my iPod. Normally listening to my favorite pieces helps me drift off, but last night it was the exhaustion of crying, trying to process the emotions of the day that finally sent me into a fitful sleep. The iPod is buried in my blanket; I tug it out, stuff one earbud into my ear, and catch the opening notes of Satie's *Gymnopédie No. 1*, a soothing match to the beauty of the morning.

Today is supposed to be my first day working at Beaches N' Cream, the ice cream parlor Evan's family owns. Even thinking his name threatens to bring the tears rushing back. In the middle of everything yesterday, I forgot that one of the reasons I was excited for this job was that we'd be working together; what if he's at the shop when I show up? I'm not expected until eleven thirty, but maybe I should get there earlier? Fill out the paperwork, set up the register, and hope Evan's parents aren't too shocked or disappointed to learn we've broken up. Would he have told them? Then again, maybe I shouldn't show up early at all, and then I can use the guise of serving ice cream sundaes to avoid talking about it altogether.

Honestly, this has to be the wildest twenty-four hours ever. Finding out my best friend and boyfriend are cheating on me with each other. Nearly being run down by a van full of guys in front of everyone at the restaurant, the stupid beating of my heart when that Asher guy started talking to me and I spotted the tattoo crawling up his arm. Having to start a job right after the owners' son breaks off our relationship. A strange and disappointing start to what was supposed to be my magical last summer of freedom.

I stretch out over my covers and check my phone, even though I know I'm not going to have any messages unless they're from Mom. Actually, she never did call or text me when she arrived at Will's like she said she would. I should probably be responsible and send her a note, so I tap out a message on the device. She responds right away.

> SHAE: *Hey, Mom. Hope you got to Canada okay. Is it snowing there?*

> MOM: *Shaeline! I totally got caught up with Will and I was tired from the flight, then we got dinner and it's been a whirlwind. I hope you're being good and have a wonderful first day at your new job!*

I consider telling Mom that I'm going to have the most embarrassing first day ever because Evan's been cheating on me with Livi, but I decide against it because she'll worry and then she'll probably call and talk my ear off until it's time to leave. I just want to be left alone with my piano and my thoughts.

SHAE: *Thanks, Mom.*

I press the button on the side of the phone to turn off the screen and shuffle my way out of the bed, the sky having changed again in just the few minutes since I woke up. The fuchsia of the atmosphere has melted into white, fluffy clouds that are thin enough not to block the brilliant Florida sunshine. This makes me smile, knowing that at least I won't be stuck in an ice cream hut in the rain; maybe there will be so many tourists and enough to do that I'll forget about Evan and Livi's existence for a little while.

As the day breaks through the long windows of the house, I head to the kitchen for a glass of apple juice. Once poured, I move to the front of the house where the piano is located, turn off the air conditioning, and open the window to let the salty breeze blow through. I'd rather be a little hot with an ocean aroma in the house than cool any day of the week.

I carefully place my drink on the side table next to the upright piano and wiggle my fingers on top of the ivory keys. I usually start with scales, but today I'm feeling like just improvising and having fun with the music. I need it.

I zip through my major, minor, and augmented scale exercises, thinking about the boys in the van again—specifically Asher and how concerned he seemed about me even though we're strangers to each other. And the more I think about him and the way his attention made me feel, the more my fingers slip away from single notes to chords, chaining together to make a quiet song that I hum along with for a little while. It doesn't have words because it doesn't need to, and I'm not particularly good at writing lyrics, but there's a distinct rhythm and tone and feeling that sinks into my bones.

This makes me feel happy—or at least as happy as someone can be after going through a very public breakup and near-accident at Barracuda's and not even getting a Frozen Rocket out of it.

After playing for an hour or more, I finally retreat back to my bedroom to get ready for day one of work. I hop in the shower quickly to do something with my beachy, knotted hair. The scent of tea tree fills my nose as I open the shampoo bottle, and suddenly I feel sick. I *can't* wash my hair with Evan's favorite scent and then show up to face him at work. I shove it back into the hanging shower rack, leaving the water running, and fumble for a towel. Water drips onto the floor as I scurry into my mom's bathroom and look through her own stash of shampoo. There's one that smells like jasmine from the same brand I like, so I grab that and try to wash away my anxieties with hot water and non-Evan suds.

I get dressed in my jean shorts and a blush-colored tank top. Thankfully, I don't have to wear a uniform at Beaches N' Cream like some people do at other ice cream shops, and for that I'm eternally grateful because I don't think I'd look very good in an oversized collared shirt. Besides, how mortifying would it be to show up looking like a sack of flour when Livi will probably be hanging around looking gorgeous and shooting smug looks at my sticky apron as it is?

Once I've tossed my phone, a can of soda, and some sunscreen into my tote bag, I leave the house and make my way down to the beach. I pause for a second at the stop sign at the end of Mermaid Avenue, humming the song from earlier in my head and looking for oncoming traffic, before crossing the esplanade past Barracuda's and toward the Boardwalk. There's sand everywhere in Emerald Beach, and the sides of the road are lined with sprinkles of beige and white that swish under my sandals until I reach the wooden slats of the tourist area.

Evan's mother, Laura Jones, is already in the shop and unlocks the door for me to come in. Plastered on her face is the same fake smile I sometimes see on the girls at Barracuda's, like they're already bored with general existence. However, underneath Laura's smile is something different, something concerning, and I immediately know that she knows about Evan and Livi and the cheating.

"Hi, Shae. Come on in. Too hot to be standing around outside."

I step into the air conditioning of Beaches N' Cream, the cottage feel of the familiar parlor surrounding me along with an icy draft. The scents of overly sweet sugar and freezer burn waft through the air. Little tables and chairs in an assortment of sorbet colors are already set up, and Laura has on a monogrammed shop apron with a smudge of soft serve in the corner.

"Hi, Mrs. Jones." I try to sound cheery as the door shuts behind me and Laura locks it again so nobody enters the shop before we're ready. "Thank you so much for this, again. It will help me pay for my books when I head to Tampa. Mom says thanks as well."

Laura clears her throat, gesturing to a booth in the back corner of the store. "Why don't you have a seat, Shae?"

I wrinkle my brow but walk with her across the squeaky board floor to a worn pink bench. "Is everything okay?"

Unlike me, Laura doesn't sit, instead folding her arms and standing beside the blue bench opposite me. She looks tense and uncomfortable. Up close, the table smells a little like bleach and disinfectant and hurts my nose. "Is there anything you want to tell me about you and my son, Shaeline?"

"I—I don't think so. I mean, he...broke up with me yesterday morning. And he's dating Livi now. But I thought he had probably told you already, since we're both going to be working here and it could be awkward."

My announcement doesn't seem to faze her. In fact, her expression grows even more taut and she rocks unconsciously further away from the table. "How about something about this booth in particular?"

Biting the inside of my lip, I think hard for a second. Did something happen here before? Did Evan and I carve our names on the underside of this table or was it a different one? I honestly can't remember, though it seems like a weird thing to be upset about.

"I don't think so, why?"

"I don't appreciate you lying to me, Shae. I already know, so there's no point."

There's a sharp pain in my stomach, like a snapping piano string. "You already know what?"

"What you two did in the shop... That the two of you snuck in here last night and were...*intimate*. I don't like assuming the worst of people, but I thought you would at least be ashamed enough to come clean when confronted with the truth."

Spit gets stuck in my throat and I very nearly choke at the accusation. Laura's accusing me of losing my virginity *here,* in Beaches N' Cream? "I'm sorry, what?" I finally gag out the words, the question getting stuck in my mouth.

"I can't believe you would think *that* could make him change his mind about your breakup. He told his father and me everything when we confronted him this morning after we saw the tape, and while I'm disappointed in him, I'm even more disappointed in you. Honestly, Shae, I thought you were better than that."

"Hold on, what tape? There can't be a tape because I wasn't anywhere near here last night! I was at home all day after Evan dumped me!"

For answer, Laura points up at a boxy little security camera stuck in the far corner of the shop, its lens trained toward this side where the booth and the cash register will both be in frame. I stare at it in dumbfounded silence for at least thirty seconds, trying to process how in the world this can be happening. How can I possibly be in a video of any kind when I never left my house?

I should tell her I want to see the tape, right? Prove my innocence. But if it's really two people doing it *on camera...* I suppress the urge to shudder. It could be anyone, right? Maybe two drunk beach campers who broke in because they had the munchies or something. It's not like the locks on this place are any good. I can tell I'm panicking because my thoughts are a jumbled mess, and my hands are starting to shake; it's all I can do to keep my expression calm.

"Mrs. Jones, I didn't—" I start, but Laura holds up a hand to stop me.

"Shae, I can't. I won't. And Evan's father agrees with me. We've hired someone else to take your place for the summer. I think it's best if we don't take you on for the position."

My whole world comes crumbling down in one fell swoop. First Evan tries to get me to hook up with him right before he admits he's been cheating on me with my best friend, and now his mother and the boss for my summer job tells me that I'm being fired before I even start because he lied about us getting it on in the shop? And somehow there's *video proof*? There's a fire brewing in my stomach, bubbling up in my throat like I've eaten too many hot wings—or forgotten to eat anything after a full day of practicing. The edges of my field of vision are blurring now, and my fingernails dig into my palms so hard I know they're leaving blood-red marks.

"This isn't fair, you haven't even asked for my side—"

"I think you should go, Shae. We're going to have to open up here in a few minutes." Laura turns to leave before twisting back again on her heel. "Don't worry, though, I'm not going to tell your mother about what you two did. You're adults and you can figure that out yourselves. I just can't have that kind of behavior on my property. Next to the windows. I mean, if someone saw..."

She stops and sighs before escaping to the back room of the shop where I know not much else is located except a few boxes of extra supplies. I think about following her back there, trying to defend myself, but I know I can't in the state I'm in right now. The summer is ruined, I'll have no money for college, and my classes and lessons and Tampa feel like they're being ripped away at warp speed. I slide out of the booth and stomp across the floor of

Beaches N' Cream. I yank at the door in blind rage and nearly pull my arm out of the socket until I realize the door's locked. I flip the lock and leave without looking back, only to run headlong into someone standing just outside the door. My sandals slip against the gritty board-walk, but I manage to keep my balance as a hand shoots out to steady me. The hand looks familiar, or at least the tattoo wrapping around the arm the hand is attached to looks that way.

Shit.

It's the guys from the sticker-covered van who tried to kill me yesterday. Somehow, they have a propensity for showing up at literally the worst times. After a breakup *and* after I get fired? Who else has that skill? And of course, it *would* be Asher, dark-haired and handsome and mysterious, grabbing my hand for the second time in less than a day.

"Hey! It's the girl who told us about Barracuda's!" one of the other guys says loudly, shouldering Asher so hard he nearly knocks him into the wall. I try to remember his name, but I don't think anyone ever said it in all the chaos yesterday.

"Shae—short for Shaeline—nice to see you again."

Asher has a gentle grin on his face that melts into a small frown as soon as he gets a close look at my pained expression. "Hey, are you okay? You look almost as upset as you did when we ran into you yesterday."

"Yeah, I mean yesterday you looked pretty, but also pretty bad," the other guy notes. He's got the same dirty-blond hair as the pushy one, but his is thick and curly instead of long and tied up in a bun. "I'm Chance," he adds with a grin that is clearly meant to be charmingly irresistible but actually seems smug. "Unlike Gabe here, I didn't try to run you over yesterday." He shoves the guy with the bun, who elbows him back.

I nod and take a deep breath, my stomach feeling all rumbly and roly-poly with the anxiety of moments ago, but also with a surprising amount of exhilaration at running into Asher and his really nice tattoos again so soon. Squeezing out a small smile, I shift us all to the side of the boardwalk away from Beaches N' Cream and lean against a yellow clothing hut, trying to look casual. "Well, I just found out I've been fired from my job, so I'm not doing too hot on top of what happened yesterday. You three know how to catch me at really bad times."

"Aw, Shae. Come get ice cream with us. Ice cream makes everything better, especially when the place name is a pun." Gabe smiles at me, a little gap between his front teeth. "We'd love to have you join us. Our treat."

"Actually," I reply, scratching absently at my neck and peeking at Asher's shoes and the fox tattoo crawling up his deeply tanned, bare leg. "Um, that's the place I just got fired from."

"Oh, shit. I'm sorry. How long did you work there for?" Gabe sounds genuinely concerned.

"Today was supposed to be my first day. But um, you know that guy I said broke up with me for my best friend? Yeah, his parents own that place and they...well, that's it, I guess." It's probably not the best idea to tell a bunch of strange guys about how my ex-boyfriend's parents think I seduced him on the table of their ice cream shop to make him take me back.

Asher frowns, opening his mouth to say something but is cut off by Gabe. "Well, guess where we aren't going, boys? We'll find somewhere else to eat. Any suggestions?"

I shrug, scanning the boardwalk for places a tourist might like, the roiling in my stomach not slowing down any as I use my peripheral vision to watch Asher's calculated movements, shifting from foot to foot in apparent thought. "There's Tin Fish for sushi, if you like that sort of thing. Pretty famous around these parts." I point over the roof of Beaches N' Cream.

"I'm down for sushi," Gabe replies, looking over at Chance, who gives a little nod like he's in on some secret joke. "But I think our boy Asher here owes you a Frozen Rocket as a thank-you for suggesting it to him yesterday. He ordered one at Barracuda's and slurped that thing down real quick. Maybe that will take the sting out of your bad day?"

Asher looks at Gabe incredulously, confirming for me there's some scheming going on between Chance and Gabe that I'm not privy to. The idea of spending time alone with a stranger I only met once for ten seconds on the side of the road seems a little bit odd, but he's an attractive stranger who has been nothing but sweet and concerned and we'll be somewhere public and...well, to be honest, I really want a distraction.

"I'd—I'd actually really like that," I admit, finally showing Asher a soft smile and looking up into his eyes.

"Perfect. We'll get out of your way and away from this puntastic parlor and meet up with you later. Maybe on the beach? I'll text you, Ash." Gabe grabs at Chance's arm and pulls him down the boardwalk, past Beaches N' Cream and off around the corner of the building toward where I pointed. The sound of the waves takes over the sound of footsteps on the wood, and soon I'm left alone with Asher.

"Barracuda's then?" he says, breaking the silence with a gentle and easygoing question.

"Sounds good to me."

We start to head back to the steps when Asher gives a quick head bob toward the ocean. "Want to walk the beach way?"

I nod, thinking about how soothing it would be to stick my feet in the cool gulf right about now. "I'd like that."

Mom and Livi and Evan would kill me for taking a beach walk and getting a drink with some boy I've known for a total of no time at all, but Mom's not around to stop me, and I don't particularly care about what my cheating friends think anymore. Ironically, it's Laura's words that come back to me as Asher and I head away from the boardwalk and step onto the hot, bright sand: I'm an adult now and I can make my own decisions. And right at this moment, I decide I'm not going to let this summer be ruined any more.

Chapter Five

ASHER

Shae looks as stunning and sad as she did underneath the Mermaid Avenue sign yesterday. Her hair has these waves like the ocean, hanging over her shoulders and halfway down her back in a dark brown that glows red and violet in the sun. She makes a brilliant first impression, and a second one at that, and as I stand there watching her talk to Gabe, I realize I'm being swept away by something about her nature. Not that you can tell everything about someone's nature within ten seconds of meeting them, but there's something in her that was worth writing half a song about at three in the morning.

We walk slowly down the steps toward the slight incline of sand, and Shae stops to kick off her sandals the second we hit the actual beach. I can tell just by the way she's moving that she's trying not to cry or explode or some combination of the two, and I don't blame her; from the little she's said, the last twenty-four hours sound like they've been hell. I slip off my flip-flops and sink my toes into the heat of the sand, wiggling them around for a second until Shae takes the first step forward.

"So, tell me about yourself," I start, trying to figure out a conversation that doesn't include me telling her I have an unexpected but immediate attraction to her aura and this kind of thing never happens to me. Gabe and Chance, sure; they've found loads of girls attractive all over the Eastern US while we've been traveling, trying to make a name for ourselves on the band circuit. But me— I'm...I don't know. Waiting for the right person, I suppose.

"What do you want to know?"

Everything, I think, but I don't say that because it won't get her talking, which is what I want. I want to distract her from the terrible things she's been going through and find out more about what she's like when she's not getting kicked while down.

"I know you said you live here. Do you go to school? Wo—" I almost ask if she works, but I remember she just got fired and cut my question off instead. "What do you like to do in your spare time? Tell me whatever you want. I'm here to make your day better."

She gives me a tentative smile. "I didn't think you'd remember anything about me, to be honest."

"I'm not sure it's easy to forget someone who was inches away from being crushed by your band van."

"True."

"And your drink recommendation made an impression too. Not many people suggest kids' drinks to me these days." I offer up a grin and Shae gives me a bigger one back. *Success*. "You still aren't talking about you though."

"Okay, fine... I've lived here in Emerald Beach my whole life. I'm going to school at the University of Tampa in the fall. Or, well, I'm supposed to." The smile fades from her lips. "The job at Beaches N' Cream was supposed to help pay for part of my tuition and my books. I only got a half-tuition scholarship and...well, we can't really afford for me to go if I don't save up over the summer. I need to find a new job in the next few days, but it's not very likely around here. Most of the summer temp jobs are already taken." Her voice is heavy and sad.

We reach the water's edge, and Shae stops for a moment to let her toes sink slowly into the wet sand, the clear blue water lapping at her feet. I do the same, but I'm paying more attention to her than the waves. Being close to the water seems to make her happier, like her emotions are going up and down with the tides as she tries to process her feelings about a summer that has totally fallen apart.

"What are you going to study at Tampa?" I say quietly as we stand there in the whisper of the breeze and the waves.

"Music. Piano Performance."

My already piqued interest suddenly skyrockets. "You're a musician?"

Shae lets out a tiny laugh, and it strikes me that I may have sounded a little bit too interested. "In the most classical sense. Didn't you just call that stickered death machine of yours a band van? Does that mean you're a musician too?"

"I'm actually here with Gabe and Chance for the Buskers Festival in Tampa. We're a traveling band in the summers and a whole lot of whatever we can find the rest of the year back home, playing shows at different venues pretty much every night."

"That sounds amazing."

"It has its moments. The money's not great, but we meet lots of cool people, stay in interesting places, always have some new story to use as inspiration for writing songs. But after a while you can't really get anywhere without an agent. That's why we applied to the festival. The Buskers gets a lot of attention from talent scouts, and if we get signed, we've got a chance to really go somewhere. This week is the only time we have to relax a bit before we're back on the road." I look down for a second and see Shae wiggling her feet around in the water, her pink toenails shining.

"What's the name of your band? What do you play?"

"This was supposed to be about you, not me," I chuckle, wading farther out into the water until it reaches the bottom of the tattoo on my calf before turning back to Shae. "But I'll allow it. We're called Collide. I play the guitar, acoustic and electric. Gabe plays keyboards and sings, and Chance plays kind of everything else—he's a jack-of-all-trades. Violin, some percussion instruments, you name it. He even has an old, banged up saxophone in the back of the van."

"Chance is the curly-haired one who made the joke about me looking pretty bad, right?" She comes out to join me, the water almost to her knees by the time she reaches where I'm standing.

I bob my head. "You got it. You'd never guess he's so talented by the way he acts when he gets around a woman."

"Some people like that sort of thing, I guess. Find it charming."

"Do you?" The question slips out of my mouth before I have a chance to catch it in my throat, and I immediately feel like an absolute idiot, though if Shae thinks I'm an idiot, she doesn't let it show. She just shakes her head.

"Not really. Not my type."

What is your type? I swallow the question back and ask a different one instead. "So classical music...like Beethoven and stuff?" It's not something I know about, but I learned a little about some of the most famous names in school.

The corner of Shae's mouth twists a bit with a suppressed smile. "Yes, like Beethoven and stuff. His music is great, but I prefer the French Impressionists."

I don't have a clue what French Impressionists are, but I also don't want to pretend I do and get caught lying. "I don't have a clue what French Impressionists are," I say, and Shae lets out another sparkling laugh.

"Well, I guess it's a bit of a misnomer, since not all of them were French. It's a period of time when composers were imitating the way French Impressionist artists were painting. Photography was becoming more popular, and artists were moving away from painting things photo-realistically and instead trying to give just the impression of things... Flowers, the ocean, people, pretty much everything." She waves a hand vaguely at the gulf. "Composers like Liszt, Chopin, and Debussy were all doing the same thing with music."

"And why do you prefer them to Beethoven?" Hopefully, that's an intelligent enough question. I'm completely out of my depth with this girl; she knows things I've never even dreamed of knowing, and it's totally fascinating.

A dreamy look comes over Shae's face. "It's in the name, isn't it? The music is full of impressions of things around us. When you play a piece like that, it's like drifting along with a current. Your fingers glide across the keys and you just...lose yourself in emotion." She closes her eyes and turns her face toward the sun, her hair rippling in the wind again, and I catch a whiff of a scent that is light and floral. "Does your music make you feel like that?" she asks, still with her eyes closed.

I think about that for a moment. "Honestly? Sometimes. When I'm writing something new, trying to figure out exactly how the lyrics in my head fit with a new melody, there will be days when I don't look at the clock until the sun is setting. Actually, I was up until three last night writing a new song and didn't even realize how late it was."

"Do you write all of the songs for the band?" Shae asks, and she seems genuinely interested, turning away from the sun to look right at me with bright, brown eyes.

"Mostly." I shrug. "Gabe has written a couple of things, and Chance is pretty good at writing riffs and tags. But yeah, I guess most of the songs are mine."

"I think that's amazing. Melodies are fairly easy for me, but I can't imagine writing lyrics. And then actually performing them in front of a real audience?" She hunches her shoulders in an exaggerated shudder. "No thanks." But she's still smiling, and she looks less burdened than she did on the boardwalk.

★

We splash around in the water getting to know each other for a little while longer, the bottoms of my shorts getting soaked and Shae's tanned arms turning darker with the afternoon sun. She tells me about her mom leaving for the summer to visit her cowboy boyfriend in Canada, of all places, about Evan and Livi, who are definitely the couple I saw in the restaurant yesterday, and bits and pieces of her senior year. Every now and then she waves at people on the beach who call her name and wave back. She doesn't shout back at them, though, and I find I like her quieter attitude. It's never very quiet around the guys, especially Chance.

I tell her about traveling around the country, what it's like to visit places with Gabe and Chance, and how I write music. Meanwhile, I can feel my skin burning, turning me into a lobster-red version of myself.

"What do you think about heading over to Barracuda's for that drink?" I suggest, looking down at my now-crimson arms.

"Whoa, yeah. Let's get inside. You're burnt. Didn't you put on any sunscreen?"

"Didn't think I was going to need it."

"It's Florida in the summer. You always need it."

Smirking at Shae, I kick a little wave in her direction, and she squeals as the cold water hits her right in the stomach. Before she can get me back, I race out of the gulf and onto the sand past her shoes and bag that she left on the beach. She doesn't give up though; she chases after me halfway to Barracuda's, and my heart pounds and I laugh the whole time. I don't know what she expects to do if she catches me, so I let her, just to see the result.

She catches up to me, hair streaming behind her back in the heat and sunlight. When we slow to a walk, her shirt sticking to her belly and the bottoms of my shorts dripping water, Shae takes a finger and flicks me right on the most burnt part of my arm.

I wince at the sting and suck in a loud breath. "Ah! Okay, I deserved that."

"You definitely did."

We put on our sandals and flip-flops and stroll up the back steps to Barracuda's together. I take a seat in the shade, but Shae doesn't. Instead, she drops her purse on an empty chair and pulls out a credit card from some hidden inside pocket. "I'll get us drinks if you let me know what you want."

"I'll pay, you don't have to worry about that." I reach into my pocket for my wallet.

"No, no. I'll get this one. You can get the ones after that. I owe you for saving my day."

I smile because she's already assuming there's going to be more than one drink, something I definitely want to be true. "Frozen Rocket. As if you have to ask."

"You liked it that much, huh?"

"Lemonade and cherry and blue? What's not to like?"

Shae saunters off toward the tiki-style bar, and I set my wallet and phone down on the tabletop. Instinctively, I poke at the home button and a message flashes on the screen, sent from Gabe a half hour ago.

> GABE: *Don't mess this up. But if you do, we're at the sushi place still having beers. I won't tell them you're only twenty.*

Snorting to myself, I tap back a quick note.

ASHER: *We're just at Barracuda's now. Frozen Rockets all around. I'm not messing anything up, but thanks for the confidence.*

GABE: *I know you hate the idea of falling for a girl while we're on the road, but this one seems special, Ash.*

ASHER: *It's been one day.*

GABE: *That's long enough.*

"Deep thoughts?" Shae plunks down two Frozen Rockets on the table and slips her card back into her bag as I place my phone down on the table next to my wallet.

"Not really. Just Gabe letting me know what he and Chance are up to. Having beers at the sushi place you suggested. They'll be happy there for the afternoon, I'm sure."

"You sure you don't want to go meet up with them or something?"

My brain runs a million miles a second. I literally would not rather be anywhere but here with her right now. But I can't say that because I'd probably scare the hell out of her. "No, no. I'm happy right where I am. Good company and my new favorite drink. I'm happy here for the whole afternoon."

Shae smiles, her expression rivaling the brilliance of the sunlight. "Me too."

We look at each other, our gazes drifting from eyes to mouths to the table eventually, and my heart bangs an erratic beat against my ribs as I watch her lick her bottom lip. It probably tastes a little salty from the breeze, and thinking about the flavor of her against my tongue makes me feel intoxicated on the nonalcoholic beverage in front of me.

Eventually—long enough that it becomes obvious we're both thinking things we aren't saying—Shae twirls her straw around in her drink and takes a long, slow drag from the bottom. That breaks the spell, and I wipe a bit of condensation from my tall glass and take a mouthful of my own. The coldness from the ice gives me an immediate, sudden headache, and I press my tongue against the roof of my mouth like my dad always taught me to when I drank something too chilly too fast.

Sighing, Shae leans back into the sun and stretches out her arms so her stomach is a little bit exposed. "This is much better than working all day at the ice cream shop. I mean, the money would have been nice, but I'll keep looking. It would have been awkward working at my ex-boyfriend's parents' shop for the summer anyway."

"Probably. I'm sure you'll find something else."

She shrugs, poking her straw in and out of her cup. "Summer jobs go pretty quickly here. But the positivity is appreciated."

"Hey, I'm here to do what I can."

"Maybe what you can do is keep me talking and distracted."

"I can do that." I fiddle with the glass absently, a little pool of water forming underneath the bottom. "Tell me something. Something you wouldn't normally tell a stranger."

A little hum escapes from her lips as she thinks, sipping at the Frozen Rocket. "That's a long list."

"You have to pick one. And I promise I won't tell anyone else."

"Okay. Here's the truth. But you have to tell me something too." I bob my head, accepting her terms, and she leans in and lowers her voice so as not to be overheard by the other patrons of Barracuda's. "The reason I was fired was because Evan's parents think they caught us on tape...*in flagrante* in the back booth of the ice cream shop. But it definitely wasn't me."

"In flagrante... You mean like...doing it?" I ask, and my face feels hotter than my sunburned arms somehow.

Shae nods, her lips pressed into a grimace. "They confronted Evan about what they found on the security tape this morning, and he claimed I talked him into it as a way to get him back. It's a total lie. I was home all day, but his mom didn't even bother to let me tell my side of the story. And do you want to know the worst part?" She pauses for effect. "I just right now realized it was probably Evan and Livi who got caught on that camera, and he's trying to pin it on me.

"Why would he do that?" I suck in a mouthful of the lemonade section of my three-tiered drink.

"So he doesn't get in trouble? I don't know. I can't even pretend that I know him anymore. I thought we were super close, you know? Told each other everything, knew exactly what we were each comfortable with, and had no need to push the boundaries too far, too fast." She shrugs and takes another sip from her drink.

"If that's really what they're doing, then they're horrible people. I mean, I've only known you for a morning, but—" I cut myself off because I'm about to go on a ramble

I'm probably going to regret. Unfortunately for me, I've already said too much, and Shae totally calls me out on it.

"But what?" She leans forward, clearly intrigued.

"I—ugh. Here's something I'd never tell a stranger. I've only known you for a morning, but it feels kind of like I've known you my whole life."

A smile cracks over her face, one she tries to hide with tightness in her jaw, but it doesn't work. And right at that second, I know that maybe in some little way, she's thinking what I'm thinking. Maybe the half-song I wrote last night won't totally be for nothing. Maybe this week off from touring will lead to something. Something that means more than a random hookup in a sandy little beach town off the Gulf Coast.

I start to envision coming back here after the festival, visiting Shae for the summer, us walking along the beach at sunset and kicking ocean water at each other until we're soaked. My imagination runs wild in the silence of the small table, the restaurant bustling around us but in an almost muted kind of way. We're the only people in our own little world, complete with multicolored drinks and strange, sudden emotions we both seem to not know how to deal with.

"I—yeah." Shae stammers, a blush creeping over her cheeks nearly the same color as my sunburn. "I know what that feeling is like."

We take sips from our respective cups at the same time, immersing ourselves in the atmosphere of Barracuda's again, and accumulating tall glasses of empty Frozen Rockets on our small table. I finally check my phone again when I'm at the bar to pick up our fourth round of drinks, and there's another message from Gabe from almost an hour past. And it's pushing five o'clock.

> GABE: *Headed back to the beach. Want to meet us by the lifeguard post?*

The blender whirs in the background as I type out my response.

> ASHER: *Sorry, just saw this now. Still there?*

> GABE: *Dude, where have you been? Are you still at Barracuda's with Shae?*

> ASHER: *Yeah. Still here. We've been talking.*

> GABE: *Ash, you've got to have dinner with her. Take her to the sushi place. Walk on the boardwalk. She's into you if she hasn't run away screaming yet, and you're obviously into her.*

I start to reply but the bartender slides the drinks across the tabletop right then, and I tap my credit card on the machine as I slip my phone back into my pocket with the other hand. Dinner might not be a bad idea. A walk on the boardwalk, avoiding Beaches N' Cream of course, would be nice. Plus, I have a million other questions to ask Shae, a thousand song lyrics rolling around in my head, and a hundred smiles telling me this girl from Mermaid Avenue is new and exciting and special.

Chapter Six

SHAE

Asher places a fresh glass in front me, complete with a black straw and yellow umbrella sticking out from the top of the crushed ice. We've been sitting here for hours, fending off the heat with glass after glass of sugary goodness, so many that I can't keep count anymore because Tali keeps coming to remove the empty ones. The last time, she raised her eyebrows at me in curiosity and amusement, a sure sign that she smells gossip in the making. I can't really blame her; meeting random guys for drinks isn't normal for the shy girl in town who knows more about Dvořák and Debussy than she does about dating, especially considering I just broke up with my one and only boyfriend and to all appearances am now on the rebound.

But I'm not rebounding. Half of Livi's boyfriends since middle school have been rebounds, and none of them ever made her feel like I'm feeling now, all tingly from head to toe and uncertain whether it's from the sugar or the warm, intense look Asher gets in his eyes when we lapse into silence. I take in every inch of this person I only met a day ago, right down to the little hole he has in one ear where he clearly used to wear some kind of earring. He feels familiar to me somehow, as though we've been coming to my favorite restaurant and drinking through their stock of flavored syrup for years instead of hours.

His life has been so different from mine, exciting in a way I could never imagine living myself. I must have asked a million questions about life on the road, touring, writing original songs and playing them for crowds nearly every night. Well, the playing for crowds part sounds terrifying to me, but there's a rhythm, a mesmerizing cadence to the way he talks that makes me wish—just for a moment—I could experience it too. I've left Emerald Beach maybe a handful of times aside from visiting the city every so often, but always with my parents and only before Mom and Dad split. By comparison, going on the road to play music with your best friends by your side and an open highway in front of you seems nothing short of amazing.

And at the end of the week, he'll be gone. Off to Tampa for his festival, then away to wherever else his band plans to go before the summer ends and they have to go back to some semblance of normal life. The thought is sobering; suddenly my stomach feels heavy and sick with the weight of disappointment and too much sugar.

"What's wrong?" Asher asks, taking his seat across the table from me.

"I was just thinking, that's all. About how you're the— the best thing that's happened to me all summer but you're only here for a week. Kind of ironic, I guess." My heart's beating at a furious tempo in my chest and I'm distantly aware of feeling shocked that those words even came out of my mouth, but I've been drinking lemonade-flavored liquid courage all afternoon. Apparently, it's made me bold.

Asher drags a sip from his Frozen Rocket, a gentle air current mussing up his thick, dark hair. "I was thinking the same thing, to be honest."

Does he really mean that, or is he just being polite? Or maybe it's something else. *He's a gorgeous touring guitarist, after all,* a snarky little voice says in the back of my head. *What's the betting that's his usual line?*

"Being on the road, though, I mean, you must meet lots of people," I say, trying to sound casual. The implication is clear in the undertone of my voice, and for a moment I feel a stab of guilt for assuming the worst. But why should I feel guilty for being cautious, especially after what I've just been through with Evan? Although…what if Asher doesn't understand that and takes offense? What if he leaves? What if it's actually possible to get drunk on sugar? Either that, or I'm way overthinking this.

Asher doesn't respond right away, instead fiddling with his drinking straw. "I know what you're trying to ask," he says slowly, "and no, I—" He pauses again, clearly contemplating something as he twists his straw around and around, sunlight glinting off the glass. "Honestly, I haven't ever done this before. I haven't felt…*connected* to anyone in a long, long time."

"Baggage?"

"Not even. Just, lack of interest, I guess. Or something else that I've never figured out." He sucks in a deep breath and lets it all rush out at once. "Gabe and Chance, they're like other guys. They meet girls everywhere and have no problem with it. Chance thinks it's practically expected that guys on tour will sleep around, jump from person to person without caring what happens afterward. But that's not me. I need...more. An emotional connection. The kind that doesn't come around very often. Does that make sense?" He looks up through his dark lashes at me, embarrassed, and the rhythm of my heart skips a beat.

"I think that's how I feel too," I say quietly.

The bell over the door inside the restaurant jingles at that moment and I instinctively glance toward the interior. All the ice in my stomach feels like it forms into a solid mass as Evan and Livi step over the threshold. Every muscle in my body tenses up and the lemonade flavor is suddenly sour on my tongue.

Asher notices the change at once and his eyes dart in the direction I'm staring. His brows wrinkle together in concern, and before I can even think of what to say, he shoves back his chair and grabs my hand. "Hope you're not too attached to that Frozen Rocket," he says in a low voice as he tugs me from my seat. "If we go now, they won't see you."

I nod and tighten my hold on his fingers. Together we hurry over to the stairs and back down onto the hot sand. My chest is tight and the heat in my cheeks is definitely not from all the sun we got earlier in the day, but the mere act of *doing* something instead of sitting like a deer in the headlights is already making me feel better.

"Where should we go?" he asks, staring around at the unfamiliar landscape. "The guys are at the sushi place, but that's all the way at the other end of the boardwalk."

"This way." Now it's my turn to tug him along after me, and I lead him over to the side of the stairs and duck under the porch boards of Barracuda's. There's the soft sound of swishing sand behind me as Asher slips a little, but he doesn't let go, just keeps his head down to avoid brushing it against the deck overhead. It's cooler here than it was up above. Little stripes of light are streaked across Asher's chest and face as we turn to face each other, and I press my finger to my lips as two familiar voices fill the air.

"Evan, come on, I don't want to sit out there today."

"Didn't you see that?"

"See what? I didn't see anything."

Footsteps thump across the deck and stop directly on top of where we're hiding. "I think Shae was here. See? That's her drink."

"So?"

"So...that's a lot of glasses for one person."

I can't help it. I let out the tiniest of giggles, covering my mouth with my free hand to try to stifle the noise. Asher's eyes are practically dancing, and his lips are pressed together so hard that they are turning white with the effort of not laughing too. This shouldn't be funny, but it is and it's dispelling all the achy nervousness of being surprised by Evan and Livi's arrival.

Livi lets out a petulant sigh. "Whatever. I'll bet her teeth are all blue like they always are when she drinks that stuff." Her voice fades as their footsteps return to the interior of the restaurant, but she talks just loud enough that I hear her next words. "She is *so* juvenile. I don't know how you dated her for so long."

That wipes the smile off my face...until Asher flashes a brilliant one of his own, displaying teeth that are tinged with just the faintest hint of bright blue. It doesn't take all the sting out of Livi's insult, but it helps a bit.

Still, I don't want to stay and hear the people I used to trust talk like that about me anymore. I tip my head toward the other end of the boardwalk and Asher nods silently. We slip off our shoes and scoot quietly through the sand until we're at the far corner of Barracuda's deck.

"We'll have to slip out and hug the edge of the boardwalk," I whisper to keep my voice from carrying. "Then we can cut back down to the water and mingle with the rest of the people on the beach."

"Want me to go first?" Asher whispers back. "Or you can slip out and I'll come right behind to block you from view."

"Let's do that."

I carefully duck out from under the porch and press my shoulder against a support pole driven deep into the sand. Asher is quick to follow; I can feel him right behind me, so close it's like he's radiating the heat of the Florida sun as I lead him away from Barracuda's with the sand slipping under our feet, aiming for a clump of tourists who are exiting Beaches N' Cream and heading out toward the water.

"We should be out of their sight line now," I say with a glance over my shoulder.

"She's wrong," Asher says suddenly, but then he stops as though he's worried bringing it up again will hurt me. When I don't burst into tears or throw him a dirty look or whatever he thinks I might do, he licks his lips and continues. "You're one of the most intelligent, down-to-earth girls I've ever met. Anyone would be lucky to date you."

My cheeks feel flushed again and I deliberately fix my gaze on his sleeve tattoo so I don't have to meet his eyes. Not that they aren't gorgeous eyes, just like the rest of him, but something in the tone of his voice makes me feel giddy and shy and a little reckless all at once.

"Shae?"

"Mhmm?"

"Do you want to have dinner with me?"

My heart skips a beat at the question, and now I can't help but drag my gaze over Asher's flexing bicep and up to his eyes. "I do."

The words feel momentous in a way I can't explain, simple as they are. Asher's lips part with one of his brilliant smiles, and my heart melts into mush at the sight of it. If he keeps smiling like that at me, I'm going to lose it. I'm going to forget all about Evan and Livi, forget about worrying over going to Tampa, forget about everything.

"Gabe said the sushi was good at the place you mentioned. We can walk over there?" Asher brushes his hair back from his face, cheeks pink from the warmth of the day.

"Can we take the long way?"

"What's the long way?"

"I'll show you."

I stuff my footwear into my tote bag and sling it over my arm while Asher holds his in his hand farthest from me. The "long way" is really just walking along the water's edge instead of the boardwalk, but Asher doesn't seem to mind. Soon we're splashing through the foamy shallows once again, and as we walk, our shoulders bump together.

An electric current forms between us, a magnetic connection, and the second our bodies touch it's as if we're immediately linked. I don't know how to describe it because it's nothing I've ever experienced before, but something tells me that this is how I was supposed to feel when I met Evan, but never did.

Emerald Beach is slowly emptying out, the tourists retreating to their condos and one of the many waterfront restaurants for supper, and I'm certain that given the time, Asher and I will have to wait for a table at Tin Fish since it's so small. But the long way down the beach takes a bit of time, and instead of cutting back up to one of the wooden boardwalk staircases, I take our stroll over to the shade of the old pier where the sand gets cooler.

"This is the long way. Also, the less hot way." I give Asher a little half-grin, the corners of my mouth quirking upward.

"It's got to be ninety degrees outside."

"Something like that, if not more. Hottest day this year so far. Don't tell me we've been reduced to talking about the weather, like the magic spell's been broken from Barracuda's?" I laugh, kicking at the lapping water around my feet and spraying droplets around us like we did earlier in the day.

"Definitely not. Ask me something more interesting."

I think for a moment, trying to make it sound like I haven't been checking him out practically all afternoon. "Tell me about your tattoos. Do you have any more other than the fox and the sleeve?"

Asher runs a hand up his inked arm, looking down at the flowers on his skin as we stroll somewhat aimlessly underneath the pier. The bustle of diners and tourists fades into a general hum above us, footsteps all melting together. "A few more. Some birds, some stars, a lyric."

"Where are they?"

Without any warning Asher stops walking, and it takes me a moment to realize he is no longer beside me. I turn and see that he's grinning softly, running the fingers of one hand along the hem of his shirt.

"Do you want to see?"

I can't think of anything I want more.

He drops his flip-flops and twists off his T-shirt to expose his broad shoulders and thin waist, the skin not as red as his sunburnt arms, then crumples his shirt in his hand as he rolls his shoulders back, allowing me the opportunity to fully take in the sight of his chest. My breath hitches in my throat as my eyes travel from tattoo to tattoo. I'm doing my best to look like I'm interested in the ink and not totally checking *him* out instead, but that's exactly what I'm doing—and I know he knows it. My gaze licks over two flying birds settled near the deep V of his hips, three stars lining his ribs, and a cursive lyric scrawled along his collarbone: *find me in the darkness under the moon.*

"What do you think?"

I reach out my hand like I'm going to touch him, but then pull back because I remember that he's a stranger and probably wants at least some semblance of personal space even though he's standing in front of me with no shirt on. "Did they hurt?" I ask instead, seizing the strap of my tote bag in a vice-like grip.

"A little. Some more than others. It hurts most when they tattoo over the bones."

I don't say anything for a minute, just looking back and forth from the designs on his body to his handsome face. "That sounds, well, horrible actually." I admit at last, crunching my own face up a little at the thought. "A needle on your bones. Ugh."

Even so, I almost wish I had a tattoo of my own to show. It's fascinating, the idea of someone's artwork on you forever, but as often as I've thought of it, even day-dreamed about what design I might choose, I've been too afraid to take the leap and book an appointment. My skin is just tan and bare and empty, and somehow it feels like a metaphor for my whole life.

★

Asher smooths out his shirt again and tugs it back over his head, interrupting my ogling and dropping me back down to Emerald Beach, Florida, on Planet Earth. His dark hair ruffles with the fabric and he skirts a hand over top of the strands to get them to lay down a bit flatter before leaning over to pick up his sandals. We start walking again, the chatter of Tin Fish above us getting closer, the Caribbean-style music that's always playing through the front door speakers slowly drowning out the noisy diners.

"That's Tin Fish up there, the sushi place." I point toward the boards above our heads, trying to shake the visual of Asher shirtless from my memory bank, even though I'd rather it stays there forever.

"I might be able to throw you over the railing if you want to take a shortcut?"

"Very funny." I bump into his shoulder again and that magnetic feeling sticks us together so much that we don't walk as far apart for the rest of the way down underneath the pier.

Dinner at Tin Fish is filled with more conversation, the sun starting to fade into the usual nighttime array of gulf colors around us. Asher and I talk underneath the fairy lights of the patio until the sky gets dark and the tea candles on the table are nothing but wet puddles of ivory-clear wax that sizzle out. Stars begin to dot the clear, ocean-like sky in blinking, milky whites, and it's only once the moon comes out and hangs over the top of the water that I realize I've spent all day with Asher, a stranger, who I met because of serendipity or fate or some other cosmic force. The air between us is warm and thick and has the whisper of salt and the sea.

We're sitting in the quiet bustle of the restaurant, the music having changed into something quieter as the place begins to empty out, looking over the pier out toward the moon when Asher asks me another question.

"Shae?"

"Yeah?"

"I think they're trying to close up here. Maybe we should go?"

I twist and look over at the empty tables with the chairs on top. We're the only ones left, and the servers are wiping down the last of the counters and open kitchen surfaces. It's later than I thought it was, but I guess I shouldn't be surprised; time seems to be on its own schedule when I'm with Asher.

"You're probably right. Let me get the bill." I go to shift out of my seat and dig in my tote, but Asher hops up first.

"I already got it earlier. Don't worry, it's taken care of."

"Just—let me know how much I owe you. I can get you the cash."

"Shae, it's my treat. You've had a rough couple of days, and I want to make it better." The way he says "want" makes it sound more like "need," and my stomach twists a little in response.

"You don't even know me, Asher. I'm just some girl from some town you're passing through." I mean the words as a bit of a joke, but they come out too real, too serious.

A pained look flits across his face, as if I've flicked his sunburn again. He doesn't reply, and I feel like I know why—because my comment is true, and yet he feels... something. The same something I feel when we get close to each other. It's intoxicating and more than a little nerve-racking.

We walk close to each other, down the lamplit board-walk past Beaches N' Cream that's long since closed for the night. I'd love to throw a rock through the window, but everyone would know it was me, and plus, there aren't any good rocks in the vicinity. Then the scent of something woodsy and citrusy wafts over me and I forget all about revenge-fueled vandalism as I realize it's something Asher is wearing.

"Where to now?" he asks after we reach the steps back by the beach.

My heart is screaming at me to invite him back to the house, to spend the night talking and breaking into Mom's liquor cabinet in the living room and watching old movies from the '90s. But my head reminds me that I told Mom I wouldn't get into trouble and having a stranger over at the house the first day I've met him seems like it would be something she would consider problematic.

"I—" I stammer. "I'm not sure what we're supposed to do next."

Asher leans against the banister in the dark, giving me an amused look. "I don't think there's any "supposed to" in this situation. I think it's a matter of what we want."

"I don't want to leave you," I blurt, the words coming from my mouth before I have a chance to filter them. My insides feel like they're all tied up in knots every time Asher looks at me, and my mouth works faster than my brain does—for the most part. It almost seems like he's having the same problem, though he looks much more calm and collected than I feel.

"You can come back to the condo if you want? But Gabe and Chance will be there. I have my own space, though, kind of like an en suite, so they won't be able to bother us too much."

"Do you really think that's a good idea? I mean—"

"Don't say it's because we're strangers again, Shae. I think we've already established that. Is there a reason you're so hung up on it?"

"It just—it seems too fast."

"Too fast for what?" He scrunches his eyebrows together in thought, sliding a hand along the railing as I shift my weight on the staircase.

I suck in a deep breath, knowing I've backed myself into a theoretical corner. I look past Asher for a minute at the seagrass blowing in the gentle air, and I let all my words fall out into the night.

"I like you. I feel something." I take another breath as I wait for his expression to change, but it doesn't. "And I'm scared that it's too soon after Evan, and too soon because it's only been a day, and too soon because you're only here for a week and then you're gone, and I might never see you again. I've never felt this way about anyone. Not after a day, not after a week, not after months and months."

Asher pushes off the handrail and takes a small step toward me. "Does that make you want to own this night, or does it make you want to forget it?"

We don't say anything for at least thirty seconds, our eyes meeting and our gaze licking over each other's silhouettes. I don't think I need to answer the question because when Asher's hand brushes my skin, I don't pull away. Instead, I softly slide my finger up the back of his thumb. He responds by wrapping his grasp around my hand so we're entwined, and we both sigh, then chuckle in unison.

"I was hoping I wasn't feeling something you weren't," he breathes into the dark. I shake my head, looking down at our touching hands, fingers, palms.

"I feel it," I reply. "I feel everything."

Chapter Seven

ASHER

I want to kiss Shae.

It's barely a day and a half since the band van almost ran into her, since we stood together at that stop sign by Mermaid Avenue, and yet I want to kiss her. I want to take her back to the condo and play the song she inspired me to write. I want to fall asleep next to her in that queen-sized bed in my en suite and never let her go.

But most of all, I don't want to scare her off. She's worried about how fast this is moving, especially with me only being in Emerald Beach for a week, and honestly, I'm kind of worried too. Everything about this is new, me falling for a girl I met on tour, wanting something deep and meaningful with someone when my time in her life will be transient at best. I didn't think it would ever happen, but it has. And I'm all bunched up inside trying to figure out the right thing to do.

My eyes meet hers, and it feels like she might be struggling with the same thought, the same conflicted feelings. How are we supposed to know which is the best choice? What will break our hearts the least? Because as crazy as it sounds, if she asked for my heart now, I'm pretty sure I'd give it to her—even knowing it might be broken in a matter of days—and that thought is thrilling and terrifying.

"Asher?" Shae sighs my name and it's both beautiful and tired, like the sun and the sugar and the sand have all started to take their toll.

"Yeah?"

"I don't want to go home. But I think I probably should. It's been—I don't know. I don't want to make any decisions right now because I feel like—like I'll make a choice I'll regret later. I know we only have a week and I know what I want right now, at this moment, but..."

"But what?" I rub my thumb over the soft skin of her hand, little sizzles of theoretical electricity zapping my fingertip at the contact.

"But it's only been a day."

"Will you think differently tomorrow?"

She shrugs. "I don't know. But it feels like I need to clear my head."

My heart sinks at the idea of leaving her alone in her house for the night, but she's right that it's probably for the best. I don't want her to regret anything or feel uncomfortable or confused about anything that might happen. All I want is her and her happiness.

"Want me to walk you home?"

"I'd like that."

We walk along the beach until we find a gate toward the street, where a single car slowly makes its way down the road with bright, white headlights illuminating the blacktop and reflecting off the double yellow centerline. I don't let go of Shae's hand as we walk across the main avenue, and she doesn't try to let go of mine. Instead, we simply stroll across the pavement toward Mermaid Avenue, the spot where I saw Shae for the first time and completely fell on my ass for her.

My gaze flicks up toward the street sign for a moment, as I try to remember the moment while we're still moving. Shae and I aren't talking or anything, just passing magnetic pulses through our hands to each other, the gravel and sand underneath our shoes making crunching noises. The waves in the distance can still be heard from halfway up the road, and soon we come to a stop in front of her house, the windows dark and a mailbox out front reading "Samson" on the side.

"This is me." Shae nods to her left and looks somewhat wistfully at the open bay window of what I assume is the living room.

"I'll at least walk you to the door and make sure you get in safely. I wouldn't want anything to happen in the twenty feet from the driveway to the front door."

She snorts, the sound making me chuckle along with her. However, Shae doesn't hesitate to lead me up to the doorway, a large, solar-powered lantern on the front step, the only source of light except for the moon and stars. The flickering fake candle makes long shadows on the stoop and they stretch away to dissolve among the grass and flower beds. Our hands are still linked, fingers now loose, and we stand facing each other as if waiting for the other to make a move.

"Asher?" She says my name like a question, and every time she does it drives me absolutely crazy.

"Shae?" I reply, trying to make my voice sound as smooth as hers.

"Thanks for today. It was really special."

The corners of my mouth turn upward in a little half-smile, and my cheeks start to burn hot. "I'm glad. It seemed like the only right thing to do. You've been hurting, and even as a stranger I could feel it, like it was my own pain in a way, you know?"

"Yeah. I know."

God, I want to kiss her so bad. The feeling is so intense that I can't think straight, can't remember what I want to say, can't figure out what my next move here should be. I know I should let her go, say good night, and head back to the condo, but something about the night feels unfinished, and my stupid brain is telling me it's because I haven't kissed her. I haven't wrapped my hands in her hair and exposed her neck and pressed my lips along the delicate skin under her jaw. I haven't pressed her up against the wall of the entryway and I definitely haven't let my fingers wander along the small of her back as she returns the kiss I so passionately want.

"Asher." She says my name again and it drops me back down to the doorstep, and she's close—closer than she was before I started thinking about what I'd do if she were ever that close to me.

"Shae?"

"You feel this, right?"

The very second I nod, Shae crashes into me, pushing her soft lips against my own like I'm the only way she's going to be able to breathe. For half a second, I'm stunned and forget my own name and where I am, but the next half-second brings me back to reality. I slip my hands around Shae's waist and up her back, twirling my fingers in the lengths of her dark waves, pulling on the strands just hard enough that she sighs into my mouth as we kiss. Instead of me pressing her back and shoulders against the wall, she steps into me, putting me just off balance enough that I have to step back and then find myself in between Shae and the entryway. Her hands crawl under the hem of my shirt, near my bird tattoos, and grasp the belt loops of my shorts as my shoulders grind into the bumps of the stucco.

She needs me, and I desperately need her.

Tugging her head back, I draw my lips away from hers and find a spot for them on her neck, where I give a gentle bite to the skin and she lets out the tiniest moan. I could listen to that sound for the rest of my life and not get tired of it, so I pepper small nibbles down her neck to her collarbone, not letting go of my hold on her soft hair that's now wrapped in between my fingers.

"Ash—" She doesn't get my whole name out before I kiss her bare shoulder with a growl in my throat. The scent of her hair is floral, exotic, and her skin smells like coconuts and lime and sunscreen. "Asher."

"Mhmm?" I loosen my clasp on her hair, but barely back away because she's still so close and I have nowhere to go.

"Maybe we should go inside?"

"I thought you said that—"

"I know what I said. I take it back. I take all of it back. Please just don't stop here. I can't—I just—don't." Her words are flustered and it's both sweet and incredibly attractive. Her face glows with the light of the lantern, accented with tiny freckles I never saw until this very moment.

"What about yesterday? And what you said earlier about being afraid of it only being a week?"

"I'm more afraid of losing what I feel right now."

I nod, lifting my head and looking straight into Shae's lamplit eyes. "I'm afraid of losing you."

"I'm not guaranteeing anything other than more of this tonight and maybe some coffee in the morning."

"That's all I need."

Shae backs away, rummaging around in her bag for a set of keys. She unlocks the door to the dark house. We walk over the threshold and the front door clicks closed behind us, the warm night wind blowing through the open window and rustling the sheer curtains. In the corner of the room is an upright piano, the bench pulled out with music books set on one side, and the only reason I can see any of it is because the moon shines perfectly through the glass to land on the polished wood.

We slip off our shoes and she brushes past me, almost purposefully touching my arm with hers, guiding me wordlessly into the depths of the house. I follow along behind, watching her move so gracefully down the hallway, past portraits of the sea on white shiplap walls. At the end of the hallway, a door squeaks open and that same moon comes through a different pane of glass, landing on a double bed with a ruffled white quilt and a fake fur rug on the hardwood floor.

Crossing the room, Shae stands alone for a moment in the moonlight. It reflects off the violet highlights of her hair and my heart begins to beat a million miles a minute again.

"Come here," she murmurs, and I don't need any more convincing to meet her next to the bed. As soon as I reach her, she sinks down onto the quilt and scoots herself into the middle of the mattress with her legs crossed to give me room. I take a seat on the edge, but seconds later, Shae crawls over to meet me, pressing a hand on my shoulder to wordlessly lay me back against the softness of the bed.

"Shae, we don't have to..." I try to remind her in a gentle way that she's only recently changed her mind from needing time to process what's happening to inviting me into her bedroom. She's probably still in a little bit of shock about what happened with her ex, and the last thing I want is for this to be about filling that void...to learn that her feelings are shallow while I'm drowning in the depths of mine.

She bites her lip and then sighs. "I just—I don't want you to leave."

"I'm not going anywhere. I'll spend this whole week with you. Hell, my heart wants to spend the rest of my life with you. Who gives a shit if it's only been a day? It's been the best day I've had in the history of my life and I want more of them. I want all of them to be with you." Better to lay it all out now, while I'm still intoxicated by her touch, her scent.

"You don't think this is stupid? The way I feel?"

I sit up, pressing my back against the headboard of her bed. "It's not stupid. I feel the same way. And I'm not just saying that. I'm just worried, like you are, that we're going to do something one of us is going to regret."

"Are you going to regret this?" she asks, rolling onto the bed and laying on the pillow next to me to stare up at the ceiling. I shift over on my shoulder.

"Never. I'm more worried about this being you trying to get over Evan by getting under someone else."

Shae laughs, the sound sweet. "That's a valid concern. But it's not about Evan. Well, I guess in one way it is because I never felt about him the way you're making me feel. I didn't know feelings could disappear so quickly and grow somewhere else just as fast."

"I don't know that they usually do."

"Maybe what we have is special then."

I smile into the dark, but I know she's watching because I feel her eyes on me. "I think you're right."

★

We stay in her bed like that for a long time, not kissing, but talking softly every so often. Whatever impulse took us on the front step has faded into something less intense but also somehow more intimate. After a while, Shae shifts closer to me, wrapping her legs over mine and resting a hand against my bicep. Even this much contact is more than I feel I can reasonably expect, and I let myself relax under her touch until I start to doze off. Shae's breathing slows down and becomes more even and then she falls asleep completely.

Eventually I rouse enough to wonder what time it is. Careful not to move too much and wake Shae, I pull my phone out of my pocket and angle the screen away from her face. The clock on the home screen tells me it's well after two in the morning, and there's a slew of unread messages waiting in my inbox, all of them from Gabe. I untangle myself from Shae and slowly pad out of her bedroom and back to the living room.

Sitting on the piano bench, I nudge a couple of music books to the seat edge and simultaneously pull up Gabe's texts on my phone. There are four, spaced about an hour apart.

> GABE: *How was dinner?*

> GABE: *Dude, where are you?*

> GABE: *Asher, don't tell me you went home with this girl already?*

> GABE: *Text me when you get this.*

I tap out a quick note, not expecting a response when it's so late, but Gabe is clearly still awake because I get one right away. Sometimes he really *is* like the parent of the group.

> ASHER: *I'm at Shae's. Long story. Well, maybe not. We like each other. It's different. I don't know how to explain it.*

> GABE: *You don't have to explain it. People search a long time for what you happened to stumble on.*

He doesn't know the half of it. Maybe I'm tired or suffering from heat stroke or something, but after a moment I type out the most prominent and possibly the stupidest thought in my head.

ASHER: *I can't leave here in six days.*

GABE: *Then don't.*

Whatever I expected him to say, it definitely wasn't that. I look up at the moon shining outside the living room window and try to make my sluggish brain think through the magnitude of what Gabe's implying. If I stay, what happens to the band? To our chances of finding an agent at the Festival? Will Shae feel different when she wakes up in the morning?

ASHER: *It's too soon.*

GABE: *Says who?*

ASHER: *Logic. Reason. My brain. Hers too.*

GABE: *Then enjoy the next six days. Decide after that. But don't tell me there isn't some kind of connection going on. You've never acted like this in all the years I've known you, not even with Sasha. And don't say I can't know because I wasn't around today. I didn't need to be.*

ASHER: *But you weren't around today.*

GABE: *Whatever, dude. I know what I saw, and I know you'd never spend all day alone with a stranger unless there was something special about her. All I'm saying is, don't get so hung up on timing that you miss out.*

ASHER: *When did you get so bossy?*

GABE: *I'm serious, Ash. There's something there that's never been there before. Don't let it go too easily.*

"Asher? Everything okay?"

I nearly jump out of my skin at Shae's quiet voice behind me. I've been so deep in my conversation with Gabe that I didn't hear her come down the hallway.

"Yeah. Everything's fine. Just Gabe wondering what happened to us tonight. I figured I should text him and I didn't want to wake you."

Shae picks up the piano books I pushed aside and moves them to the coffee table, then sits next to me on the bench, turned toward the piano but with her hip pressed close against mine. She doesn't say anything, but she opens the lid and pokes at the keys, lacing together soft tones under the moonbeams. "I wrote a song the day I met you, you know. Well, I didn't write it down. It's in my head."

I sweep my gaze over to her, incredulous. "So did I. Well, half of one."

"Can I hear it?"

"I don't have my guitar."

She nods, trickling her fingers over the keys to play a series of beautiful notes that take over the living room and cascade out of the window into the silent air. "Tomorrow night?"

I lean my arm into her shoulder. "It's already tomorrow."

"I guess it won't be long to wait, then."

Chapter Eight

SHAE

The sound of birds wakes me up late in the morning, and I half expect to roll over and find myself alone in bed. But Asher's still here, twisted in my sheets with one hand tucked behind his head as his chest silently rises and falls to the rhythm of his breath. His shirt is off and crumpled on my nightstand; the lines of his tattoos seem somehow sharper than the day before, as though a night of kissing and cuddling has imprinted their patterns on my mind. I want to reach out and touch the one on his collarbone, gently waking him up, but then it strikes me that I haven't brushed my teeth or hair since yesterday. What in the world must I look like?

I roll lightly off the bed, sneak out through the open doorway, and creep down the hallway to the bathroom where I tie my knotted hair up in a ponytail, brush my teeth, and wipe down my face with witch hazel toner. I stare at myself in the mirror for a few seconds and consider putting on a little makeup to cover the old acne scars on my cheeks, but then I reconsider. Asher liked me yesterday when he could see them. Why wouldn't that be true today?

The clock in the hallway tells me it's fifteen minutes to noon. I slip back into my room and manage to crawl back under the quilt just as Asher stirs and opens his eyes. The first thing he does is grin and stretch, his arm muscles rippling.

"Morning." He shifts his weight on the memory foam and adjusts his position so he's on his side facing me. "How'd you sleep?"

I rub at my cheek, brushing away a stray hair from my ponytail. "Good. It was...different, having someone in bed with me. I hope I didn't kick you or anything," I add with a glance at the twisted sheets.

"You definitely didn't kick me. You stayed on your side and I stayed over here, and we were proper adults about the whole thing." Asher chuckles, running his free hand along the side of his hair where it's all mussed up. "Do you typically kick bed partners in your sleep?"

"Bed partners? Really? You can just ask if I've ever kicked Evan in my sleep. His name isn't poisonous. But the answer would be no because Evan and I never shared a bed. Not all night, not like this."

A light comes into Asher's face even as he gives me a surprised look. "Never?"

"No. Why, is that weird?" If he hadn't told me yesterday that he doesn't like casual relationships, I might be more worried about what he'll think of me for not having had any.

"Just a little surprised, that's all. I'd have thought guys would be lining up to date someone like you. Didn't think I'd be the first one. You know, as a stranger." Asher's dark eyes sparkle a little in the sunlight, like he's pleased to have found out this fact but doesn't want to say it.

"I did say I understood your feelings about intimate relationships, didn't I?" I poke him playfully in the ribs with a finger and he jerks to the side, still grinning. "What about you? Needing a connection to someone first doesn't mean you haven't had it happen at least once already."

The light fades from his face and I feel him stiffen a bit, close as we are to each other. "There was one girl I thought I might feel that way about. But she thought it was taking too long and...decided to find someone who would give her what I couldn't."

A rush of aching fills my chest. No wonder he's been trying so hard to make me feel better; he knows what it feels like to have someone you care about break your heart. He isn't looking at me now, not exactly. His eyes are unfocused and he's fiddling with the edge of the quilt binding, thoughts clearly tuned to his past.

"I'm sorry. I didn't mean to bring up old memories." My instinct is to touch him again, but should I when it's my fault he's remembering things he must want to forget?

Asher shrugs. "It's okay. It's stupid to still be bothered by it. That's what Chance would say, anyway. Gabe might get it a little."

I sit up and prop myself on one elbow. "Then Chance sounds like a real jerk. It's not stupid to have a hard time moving away from things that hurt you. Besides, what does he know about it when he spends all his time hooking up with random girls while you're on tour?"

"Good point." Asher props himself up on his elbow, too, exposing the star tattoos on his side and part of his broad chest. "For the record, nothing ever happened with my ex, either, and I haven't felt a strong emotional attachment to anyone I've met since. Well, not until..."

He pauses, giving me a crooked smile.

"Not until what?" I ask, my fingers tingling with the need to touch him, to run my hands over his sunburnt skin with the gentleness of someone who doesn't want to make his body sting but rather wants to make it feel good.

"I think you know not until what," he sighs, reaching over to me, running a hand along my bare arm. It sends sparks up my back, and I can't help the shiver that shoots through the nerves around my spine. Apparently, the shiver was too much, though, because Asher immediately pulls his hand back. "Sorry. Do you not...?"

I shake my head, instantly regretting that he took my reaction the wrong way. "No, no. It's just...every time you touch me, I feel like I'm getting shocked. It feels strange, but good. It probably doesn't make sense, but I've never felt that feeling with anyone before."

He nods, sliding his fingers down my bare arm again, stopping when he reaches my thumb. "Give me your hand. I'll show you something I like."

I let Asher take my hand, and he pulls me closer, gently lifting my arm so that it's resting on his neck with my fingers grazing his hairline. There's no helping myself; the second I run my nails along his hair, he lets out a little, low growl and I feel his body tense.

"Do it again. Harder."

I scoot closer to where he's lying and draw my hands through Asher's dark hair using more pressure than I did the first time. He sucks in a deep breath, his eyes half-closed, and I run my fingers down his neck and across his chest, leaving thin red lines on the skin.

"Am I doing it right?" I ask, tracing the lines of his lyric tattoo on his collarbone with one nail. "Do you like it?"

"I like you, Shae. You can't do this wrong."

I draw shapes on Asher's upper body with my fingers for a few minutes in silence, avoiding his sunburn, only the occasional sound of him sighing breaking through the birdsong and the breeze. Making him happy makes me happy, and as he exhales, I find I'm shaking a little with residual feelings and emotions and the electricity of touching him so intimately. When I finally bring my hand away, thinking maybe Asher's fallen back asleep, his eyes peek open at me and he grins.

"That was—there are no words for you, Shae."

Falling back on the bed and my pile of pillows, I smile up at the ceiling and let out a little laugh.

"What's so funny?"

"You're definitely not what I expected to happen to me this summer. It's wild. It's absolutely wild how fast the world can change."

"I know."

The quiet air suddenly splits with the sharp sound of someone knocking on the front door of my house. It's so unexpected that I jerk and sit up in a panic, my heart racing. Wild thoughts course through my mind. What if it's Mom, come back from her trip? She's going to flip if she finds me alone with a strange guy in my bed. Then my reason catches up with me. Of course, it isn't Mom; she'd have called if she was coming home early.

"Are you expecting someone?" Asher asks, sitting up, too, and reaching for his shirt.

"Shhh!" I wave a hand at him, trying to decide what to do. I could answer the door, but what if whoever it is decides to stay and chat? What's the chance it's one of my other friends who's heard about my breakup with Evan? Second to Mom coming home, having Marley or Jessica catch me in bed with Asher would be terrible. Especially since they saw us walking on the beach together yesterday; word would be sure to get back to Evan and Livi... Hell, to the whole town!

There's another knock on the door, silence for a few seconds, and then a voice calls through the wood. "Shae? Are you there?"

"Evan," I mouth silently to Asher, and his eyebrows draw down with his frown.

"C'mon, Shae, I know you're home!" Evan calls. "I just want to talk, all right?" He falls silent, and I can picture what he must look like standing on the front step.

Then my heart skips a beat as I hear a rustling outside. Evan is coming around the side of the house. Without a word, I shove Asher flat on the bed and fling the covers over both of us as well as I can. Apparently, he's figured out what's going on, too, because he yanks the pillow out from under our heads and pops it out of the blanket to sit on top as though I've made my bed and left the house empty.

We squish together and press ourselves as flat as we can against my memory foam mattress as the rustling sound stops outside my open window. There is silence for several agonizingly long moments while Evan stands there, probably trying to crane his neck for a view of every part of my room. My bed sits between two windows, so as long as we hold very still, he shouldn't have a great view of the blankets.

"Shae?" Evan says, and his voice is so close that for a wild moment I worry he's gotten into my room somehow and is about to discover my ruse.

I close my eyes and think hard. *Please leave...just leave... I don't want to talk to you anymore... I'm not here... Go away...*

At long last comes the sound of Evan pushing through the bushes again and then silence. Asher and I both seem to have the same idea because neither of us moves to push the blankets away for at least another thirty seconds.

"Do you think he's gone?" Asher finally asks in a whisper.

"I think so." Then the ridiculousness of the situation hits me, and I start to giggle. "Still think I'm not juvenile?" I manage to squeak out between laughs.

Asher doesn't answer. He's laughing too.

Eventually our laughter fades away and we're just lying on my bed looking at each other. Asher's eyes are so warm and full of contentment that it sets my heart beating hard again. Evan *never* looked at me like this, not once while we were dating, not even the night we got in trouble for staying out late because we were making out under the pier. He never made me feel this tingly from head to toe either.

"Asher?" I say quietly.

He knows what I'm going to ask. Slowly he rolls onto his side and lifts a hand, this time touching my face, coming close and pressing his lips gently against mine.

★

It's almost two in the afternoon by the time Asher finally sighs and swings his legs off the side of the bed. He stretches his arms high, and I watch as his back muscles furrow and reach. There's a strange sensation inside me, an aching in the pit of my stomach that makes me want to grab him and pull him back into the bed. We've been kissing for two hours and yet I'm not tired. Part of me feels like I could kiss Asher forever and never be tired of it.

"Going somewhere?" I ask in what I hope sounds like a playful tone.

He turns his head, grazing his hair again with his palm, trying to make it lie flat. "Thinking I should probably put in an appearance at the condo, just to make Gabe stop pestering me. And I probably don't smell great either. How about I go over there for a quick shower and then meet you back at the beach?"

I snort, thinking about how burnt he is already. "I think you need to stay away from the beach today, Ash. You're still awfully red."

Asher looks down at his arms. "Okay, maybe you're right. How about I meet you back here then? We can...I don't know. Something. Think of something you want to do, and we'll do it. That is, if you're not tired of me or regretting anything?"

"I'm not. To either. I'm this close to suggesting you—" but I stop because the idea of him showering in my bathroom is awkward...and maybe a *little* too tempting.

He stands, pulls his wrinkled shirt off the nightstand and over his head, giving me a knowing half-smile that shows a dimple on one cheek. His phone was underneath the shirt and is blinking with unread messages we've been purposefully ignoring. "I'll be back soon. I'll bring my guitar and play you that song I wrote, like I promised. You owe me a song on the piano, too, if I remember correctly."

My face grows hot at the memory of my admission to having written a song about Asher, but I nod. "Fine. Tonight. When it's dark and you don't have to see my face while I play. I'm not good in front of an audience unless it's Mom."

"But you're going to Tampa to study piano performance?" Asher smooths out his shirt as best as he can, though the wrinkles persist.

"I know. It sounds ridiculous. Maybe playing for you will help me get over it."

"I'm sure you're great." His voice is so encouraging that I almost believe him. "How about this? We'll have dinner, wait for it to get dark, and make music. Sounds like the perfect rest of the day to me. I'll text you when I'm on my way back."

"You don't have my number."

"Sounds like you'll have to give it to me, then." He grins, picks up his phone from the table, and swipes his finger across the screen to unlock the device.

"It's 555-3313."

Asher taps the number into what I presume is his contacts list, pokes his finger at the screen some more, and then pushes the button on the side of the phone to turn the screen black. A second later, my phone dings from somewhere underneath my pillow. "There, now you have my number, too, just in case you change your mind."

"I'm not going to change my mind."

"Neither am I."

With that, Asher disappears out of the bedroom doorway, and I hear him walking down the hall toward the front door. Moments later, there's the telltale click of the latch, a squeak, and then he's gone. All that's left with me in the bedroom is the scent of the beach, the woods, and something like tangerines.

I slip my hand underneath the pillow and pull my phone out to see Asher's text waiting in my inbox. I open it expecting to see the basic "hello" people usually use when sending someone their number, but instead find a question.

ASHER: *I miss you already. Do you miss me?*

He wrote that even before he left. The thought makes me grin like an idiot, and I curl my toes under the blankets, rubbing them against the fabric contentedly. Sinking back on the pillows, I tap out a reply.

SHAE: *I do. The bed feels empty.*

ASHER: *You're not supposed to be in bed. You're supposed to be getting ready to meet me later.*

SHAE: *Good thing I'm already at the place I'm supposed to meet you. But fine, I'll get up. I need to check the fridge to see what we can possibly eat for dinner.*

ASHER: *Don't worry about dinner. I'll bring something. You just take care of getting you ready. I'll be back soon.*

SHAE: *See you soon.*

I plunk the device down on my bed, drawing in a deep breath before I manage to will myself into taking a shower. Staying cuddled under the sheets that smell like Asher is much more appealing, but if he's going to come back fresh and clean, I don't want to be the one who kills the mood. Mom's jasmine shampoo is still sitting next to the tea tree one in the shower caddy, and I get a sense of grim satisfaction from pulling out my old favorite and tossing it in the trash, picturing Evan's face on the label covered in big, fat quarter rests that put a final stop on our relationship forever.

The warm water feels good running through my hair, and I think about the way Asher's fingers wrapped in the strands, and the very moment I decided I needed to kiss him on the front porch more than I needed anything else in the world. The memory makes me tingly all over, and I smile into the shower stream, getting a mixture of water and shampoo in my mouth that I have to wash out.

My phone is blinking with a text when I get out of the shower, toweling my hair dry. I snatch it up eagerly but my stomach sinks when the name on the screen isn't Asher's. It's Marley, and her message is short:

MARLEY: *Hey, are you home?*

It's not unusual for her to ask that, but Evan's unexpected appearance on my doorstep has me feeling wary. I type a response I hope won't give away the sudden nervous twisting that's invading my gut.

SHAE: *Yeah, just got out of the shower. What's up?*

> MARLEY: *Lots of weird stories going around this morning. Just wanted to swing by and see how you're doing.*

Marley didn't say *who* was spreading the weird stories. My stomach does a backflip. Does that mean she suspects something to do with Asher? Or maybe it's Evan and Livi, telling our friends their side of the breakup story and making me look like the bad guy in all of this. Then I remember the video tape that Evan's mom claimed I was in and it feels like I no longer have a stomach at all. Laura was so embarrassed by that video she wouldn't dare *gossip* about it...would she?

Suddenly the perfect little bubble of a world I've been living in with Asher pops in a cascade of thin, soapy film.

> SHAE: *I'm not really in the mood for visitors right now.*

> MARLEY: *No visitors. Just me, promise.*

> MARLEY: *I know you lied about not being home when Evan stopped by earlier.*

That does it. I need to know what she's being told, even if it doesn't make things better. I glance at the clock in the hall. Asher hasn't been gone long and probably won't come back before Marley leaves, as long as I get her over here right away. There should be enough time.

> SHAE: *Fine. You can come over now.*

> MARLEY: *Be there in five.*

I dress quickly and sit on the piano bench to wait for her, all thoughts of practicing my song for Asher as dissipated as my soap bubble of a day. The Debussy is still sitting on the music rest where I left it two mornings ago. Maybe practicing that would make it look more like I'm doing okay, and Marley will leave sooner.

There's barely time for half the piece before there is a loud and persistent knocking on the front door. I sigh and get up to let Marley in. She flows through the door smelling like sun, ocean, and tanning oil, a towel sticking out of her beach bag and a pair of sunglasses pushed hastily onto the top of her head.

"Hey," she says with a sympathetic smile and sets her bag down on the hall floor. "Got any water? Derek drank all mine." She rummages in her bag and pulls out an empty water bottle that she shakes for my benefit.

"Yeah."

Together we make our way to the kitchen where Marley fills up her water bottle at the sink and I plop down on a tall bar stool across from her. She keeps me in her sight line as she draws a few long sips from the bottle and then fills it up again. The temptation to fidget is strong, but not because I feel uncomfortably sad. More like uncomfortably eager for her to leave and Asher to come back.

Finally, she finishes tightening the lid of her water bottle and sets it down. She spreads her hands on either side of the sink. "Okay, girl, dish. What's been going on with you and Evan?"

"What do you already know?"

"Livi says you guys broke up. Evan says there's some kind of misunderstanding going on and he just wants to talk through it with you."

I shrug as casually as I can manage. "Sounds like you know all about it, then."

Marley's eyes narrow to thin brown slits. "So...you're not with Evan anymore? I don't have to make Derek pound his head in the sand for cheating on you with Livi at the bonfire last night?"

The bonfire... I'd forgotten all about the plan to have one, I was so caught up with Asher. At least that explains why we weren't noticed by any of my friends at Tin Fish. A little piece of me had wondered about it at the time, but it was too easy to ignore it when Asher's dark-blue eyes and muscly arms were taking up all my attention.

"No, we broke up the other morning at Barracuda's, so technically he wasn't cheating on me last night."

"Implying that he was cheating on you before that." She makes it a statement, not a question, and then lets out a frustrated snort of disgust before I can answer. "That shit. I should have Derek pound him anyway. Him and Livi. Derek's dumb enough that I could goad him into hitting a girl with enough of the right incentive." Her lips split into a mischievous smirk. Unlike me, Marley has never been reluctant about getting physical with her boyfriend. Sometimes I wondered what it would be like if I were more like her, but never long enough to worry that Evan was upset with me for going slow. At the time I'd believed him when he said he didn't mind waiting. The video tape from Beaches N' Cream clearly suggests otherwise.

"Maybe I should have made you my best friend instead of Livi," I say in a joking tone. The happier I look, the less miserable Marley thinks I am, the sooner she'll feel like she can leave. Asher won't be back nearly this soon, but the idea of his return is looming over me and making me anxious to have the house to myself again.

Marley laughs. "No kidding. I'm available now if you're taking applications and don't mind long-distance friendships." Then her expression grows serious again. "But you're doing okay?"

"I am now. The first night was hard, but I realized there's no point moping over cheaters."

"You sure didn't look like you were moping yesterday morning on the beach."

She says the words in such a normal, offhand way that it almost catches me off guard. But I see the way she's looking at me through her thick lashes, a mixture of curiosity and teasing suspicion that tells me she knows I was with a new guy. My throat goes dry and it's all I can do not to jump up and push her back down the hall and out of the door.

Instead, I shrug again and cover my embarrassment by standing up to get a cup from the cupboard. "It's nothing, really. Just someone I met on the boardwalk who was a nice distraction." Asher is absolutely *not* nothing or *just* a nice distraction, but Marley won't understand that.

"Did you guys do it last night?"

"No! Of course not!" But I'm clearly blushing now because my face feels like it's been lit on fire. "I never did with Evan, and we were together for three years, you know that."

"I'm just teasing!" Marley lifts her hands in a mock-defensive gesture but she's grinning. "I know that's not who you are. But good for you, flirting with someone the day after your breakup. I didn't think you had it in you, but I'm glad to be wrong. It'll make things easier. That's how Derek and I got together after Luke dumped me. Amazing how much it helps, huh?"

"Yeah, amazing."

"'Kay, well, Derek and the others are meeting me at In the Nood for dinner tonight. Wanna come? I told him we're not speaking to Evan anymore, so no chance you'll bump into him."

I shake my head, trying not to be too quick about it. "I think I'll stay in tonight. Mom's supposed to call from Canada and I don't want her to feel like she has to rush because I'm out with friends." Thank goodness it's a plausible white lie.

"Fair enough. And Shae, I'm glad you're okay." Marley gives me a quick hug and then I walk her back to the front door. "Offer stands if you get lonely and change your mind!" she calls over her shoulder as she and her bag swing down the front step.

"You got it!" I call back, then make myself count to ten before I close the front door and bolt it shut again.

My heart is racing like I've just run two miles on the beach or barely escaped something. Marley's words are rolling around in my head like jumbled marbles. *Glad you're flirting...didn't think you had it in you...not who you are...do it last night...* Something about those words, and the fact that I didn't-quite-but-also-kinda-did lie to Marley has me feeling weird again. Is that all Asher thinks I was doing, just flirting with him? Is that all he was doing with me? Maybe all that talk about needing a deep emotional connection was just the line he uses to pick up girls who won't be bought by his friend Chance's more brutish behavior. Maybe he was just trying to get me in bed and is only coming back because he didn't get all the way with me last night. Maybe he's just the same as Evan and Derek and all the other guys I've ever known, only interested in physical satisfaction...

I need something distracting, *now*. My piano is the first thing my gaze latches on to and I dive for it, practically slamming my fingers against the ivories and losing all sense of the elegant, flowing rhythm of Debussy's writing as I try to ignore the sinking sensation in my stomach.

Chapter Nine

ASHER

Gabe and Chance get back to the condo while I'm still in the shower and Gabe, at least, is waiting for me when I come out of the bathroom, trailing steam and water and the smell of tangerines.

"So?" he says, eyebrows raised with anticipation. He's perched on a kitchen chair with a half-eaten apple in his hand. Chance is flopped on the sofa in front of the TV with the volume up way too loud.

"So what?" I say back as I run a towel over my still-wet hair.

"He wants to know if you got some last night for a change," Chance calls over the noise of whatever show he's watching.

Gabe rolls his eyes at his cousin but lasers in on me again. "I wasn't going to be that abrasive, but..." He shrugs to finish the sentence.

Of course, all they care about is whether I slept with Shae or not, and not about all the things we talked about, the feelings we shared, the way her hair ripples in the sunlight or how her brown eyes glow when she laughs. None of the things that held me spellbound last night and kept me in bed with her all morning even though we never went beyond kissing.

"This is why I don't let you write the songs." I chuck the balled-up towel at Chance as hard as I can. "All you'd write about is sex, and we'd never get another gig."

Chance dodges away from the damp towel and then sinks back into the sofa cushions again. "Told you," he says to Gabe. "Dude chickened out."

"You're one to talk, Mr. Couldn't Close the Deal Last Night. At least Asher was making out with a girl. All you did was get drunk and throw up all over that waitress."

I'm so glad I was with Shae last night and not out with my bandmates. I've seen Chance throw up more times than anyone ought to and it's never pretty. "Sounds like a fun time," I say sarcastically, and this time Gabe rolls his eyes at me. "Did you also eat all the food? I'm starving."

"There are some leftovers in the fridge. We found a nice Thai place further into town."

"In the Nood," Chance says with a lurid chuckle.

"Funny." My tone says it's anything but funny to me. Thai food does sound good, but not after knowing it's leftovers from two guys who were around vomit last night. Maybe that's where I'll stop and pick up dinner for Shae when I go over.

Gabe gets up and scoops my used towel off the floor, then follows me back to my room. "So, are you going to see Shae again?" His voice is lowered so Chance won't hear.

"We're meeting up later." It feels weird to admit even that much, but I don't want a repeat of Gabe's constant texting. It was a real mood killer until I put my phone on silent. And I don't really know how much I want to talk about Shae—with Gabe or with anyone just yet. True, the guys are the closest thing I have to family these days apart from a deadbeat rocker uncle back at home, but we're not so close that I'll just spill everything I'm thinking and feeling to them. Maybe romantic relationships aren't the only ones I'm bad at.

"Good, that's good." He nods, but he's twisting the towel in his hands like he's got something else on his mind. "Listen, about what I said last night...when you texted...I was pretty hammered, and I don't think I was thinking very clearly."

"You mean when you said I should stay here with Shae if I liked her that much?"

He nods again. "Yeah, that. I mean, listen, I'm really happy for you and all, it's just that, well, the band needs you. We wouldn't have gotten our spot in the festival without your songs. If you leave, it won't be the same."

Leave the band? "Dude, that's *way* overboard. I barely met Shae two days ago, she hasn't got me wanting to quit the band or anything. I just meant that, you know, we don't really have any gigs planned for after the festival so maybe it wouldn't be the worst thing to kick around here for a bit, see if we can play some local bars or something."

Gabe looks genuinely relieved; all the nervous tension drains out of him like he's wilting. "We could probably manage that. Sorry," he adds quickly, "I just got worried and wasn't sure, you know? This hasn't ever happened before, and I want to be there for you, but the band is...*everything* right now. I've got nothing against serious girlfriends if they understand that."

"Well, Shae and I haven't known each other long enough for her to be a serious girlfriend, so you don't need to worry."

"Thanks, man. Hey, have fun with her tonight. Tell her I said hi, and I hope her day is going better than yesterday." Gabe goes back into the kitchen, leaving me with the towel and too many confused thoughts.

Would I consider leaving the band for the right girl? The question has never come up before for any of us, not even when I was dating Sasha. But then Sasha never made me feel the way Shae does, like I'm caught in a thunderstorm where lightning is laced into every drop of rain that fizzles against my skin. Maybe the question I should ask myself is whether I'd be willing to give up the band, the touring life, to stay here in Emerald Beach, or to move from my crappy bedroom in my uncle's house to Tampa while Shae goes to school.

Or maybe Shae would be willing to come on the road with us. Not the whole time, but during the summers maybe, when she's not taking classes. Maybe she could help with the equipment or handle our nonexistent publicity stuff—something to keep the guys feeling like she was contributing rather than dragging the band down. But would she be able to? Would she even want to? She seemed interested in the tour life yesterday, but that could change once she realized it would mean leaving home.

One thing at a time, I tell myself and start looking for a fresh pair of socks to wear with my Converse.

★

Soft piano music is drifting through the open window when I finally reach the house on Mermaid Avenue, carrying a plastic takeout bag with the food I've brought. My stomach is twisting in nervous knots; what if Shae doesn't actually want me to come back? Last night was too good, too natural to be true, but I desperately want to have another night just like it. The guitar case tugs at my shoulders as I walk up the front steps and hesitatingly put out a fist and knock on the door.

The music stops and a moment later Shae is there, her long hair swishing against bare shoulders, eyes searching my face. "Come in," she says, backing up to make room for me in the doorway.

I push through as carefully as I can. "I brought food. Gabe told me about a Thai place that's supposed to be good. There were a lot of people when I went, so it must be pretty popular. Hope that's okay. I mean, you've probably had it before. I don't know why I'm telling you about it."

Something must strike Shae as funny because she looks like she's trying to hold back a laugh. "That would be In the Nood. A lot of the guys like to go there and make jokes about the name to their girlfriends. My mom hates it, but she's also addicted to their Pad Thai." She shrugs and holds out a hand for the bag, which I give her. "You can leave your guitar by the sofa if you like. I thought maybe we could eat out on the deck."

"Sounds nice." I swing the guitar case off my back and lean it against a coffee table in the middle of the room.

Shae leads the way to the kitchen and shows me where to grab a couple of plates and some glasses, as well as a pitcher of lemonade in the fridge. The awkward feeling I had when I arrived comes back a bit as I pull open cupboards like I own the place, but it fades once we're outside on a raised stone patio overlooking her backyard. Some ancient-looking wicker furniture is arranged in a semicircle around a low glass-topped table. Together we set out the things we've brought from inside and open the takeout containers. There are chopsticks and packets of both sweet chili and sriracha sauce; the noodles smell so good that my stomach rumbles a little too loud.

"Hungry?" Shae asks, teasing, as she pulls one of the faded blue cushions off a patio chair and plops it down on the stone. "Mom and I always skip the chairs when we eat outside. The table's too low to be useful otherwise."

I grab a second cushion and toss it next to hers. "Fine by me."

"Sorry if it's a bit dusty. I tell Mom every summer that we should finally throw these out and get something new, but she insists they're still perfectly usable and won't get rid of them until they either fall apart or Nature decides to take them away in a hurricane."

The image of a wicker loveseat flying through the air pops into my head, and I laugh, which makes Shae's lips curve upward in a genuine smile, and just like that, it's as though we haven't been apart for several hours. We dig into the noodles in comfortable silence, watching the sun sink slowly toward the Gulf through a sky smeared with yellows, oranges, and pinks.

"Drat!" Shae exclaims, grabbing for a napkin from the stack that came in the takeout bag. "I guess I forgot noodles aren't terribly good date food." There's a little nest of them rolling off her leg where they dropped from her chopsticks.

"We're sitting on the floor. I don't expect anything about this to be dignified."

That makes her chuckle a little, and then she laughs outright as a moment later a huge bite of my own portion drops onto my lap too. "Please don't tell me you did that just to make me feel better."

"Never."

She hands me a napkin. On an impulse, I grab her wrist instead and pull her in for a kiss. Just a quick one, nothing too invasive, but even that quick touch of her lips against mine sparks like a live wire and leaves me a tiny bit breathless as she draws back.

"Too soon?" I say, because she's giving me a look that I can't quite interpret but doesn't seem as happy as the one she wore when I left her this afternoon.

She bites her bottom lip. "I'm not sure."

Great... Of all the times for me to decide that I want to be impulsive about physical intimacy things like kissing. "I'm sorry. I didn't mean to make you uncomfortable."

"No, it's—I mean, I liked it." But she looks away and stuffs some more noodles in her mouth as though she doesn't want to talk about why she's suddenly feeling awkward.

If I could kick myself, I would. Shae told me only this morning that we share a difficulty with being close to people we don't know well, and here I am acting as though everything I said about how I feel is a lie. How many times have I wondered if someone was putting on an act just to get something from me? She probably feels like that now.

Shae finishes eating and gets up, drags her cushion back to the chair she took it from, and sits down to face the distant ocean view. I've still got a few bites left, and somehow it feels wrong to sit as close to her as the chair would put me until we've figured out whatever it is that I can do to make her happy again.

"My friend Marley came to see me today," she says suddenly, her voice a little higher than usual. "She saw us on the beach together yesterday."

I swallow a mouthful of noodles and consider my words. "Does that upset you?"

Shae reaches up and gathers a handful of hair, drawing it over her shoulder and fiddling with the ends. "Not exactly. Not at first. But the way she talked about it made me feel weird. She said..." She takes a deep breath and lets it all rush back out again. "She called it flirting, like there was nothing serious or momentous going on and, I don't know, it made me nervous. Like maybe I've been reading too much into how quickly everything is happening."

"And it didn't help that I just kissed you out of nowhere."

The tiniest of smiles creeps across her lips. "Was it that obvious?"

"Only because I was kicking myself the second you pulled back. I wouldn't like it if someone sprang that on me either."

"I just want to make sure that I'm not running headlong into something I'm going to regret. That what I— what *we* feel is real."

I set my empty food container down, grab my chair cushion, and place it on the seat next to hers. "That's what I want too."

We sit together quietly and watch as the sun slips beyond the horizon, and somehow without noticing when or how it happens, I find that Shae has draped her arm over mine on the armrest and that our fingers are twined together. Her hand is soft, and her fingers feel thin but strong, probably from so many years of piano practice. She catches me looking at her and smiles, leaving her hand in mine. Apparently, she's forgiven me for my hasty kiss earlier, at least enough to be okay with holding hands in the salt-scented evening humidity.

"You know," I say after a while. "I'm nervous to play the song I wrote for you."

Shae bites her bottom lip again, squeezing my hand softly. "Me too. It feels so intimate. More than what happened yesterday. Not that I'm trying to downplay the way yesterday made me feel—"

"I know what you mean." I squeeze her hand as well.

She turns back to watch deep indigo seep like ink across the sky overhead. "We've shared a lot in just a couple of days, but sharing my music is like baring my soul. Is it not like that when you're playing concerts?"

"Not exactly. Playing in a bar or at a waterfront is just another show. Get up, play a few songs, flash a smile to an audience who doesn't care if it's real or fake." I fix my gaze on our joined hands. "But playing a song I wrote for a girl I just met is different. It's...everything, I guess. One of the last things I have to show you about me. Like I'll have..." I let the sentence hang, unfinished, in the air between us.

"Like you'll have what?"

I shift in my chair so that I'm facing her, and she meets my eyes with her own. "Like I'll have nothing left to offer after the music. Like you'll have every part of me."

Shae doesn't say anything for a long time, just sits there holding my gaze and thinking her own private thoughts. Then she uncurls herself from the wicker chair and stands up, tugging at my hand. There are stars appearing in the sky overhead like diamond pinpricks floating in her long hair.

"Play something for me?"

I take a deep breath in, hold it for three seconds, and let it puff out all at once before I respond. "Okay."

She leads me back through the house to the front room where her upright piano stands in a puddle of light from the streetlamps, the curtains billowing around it in the nighttime air like long fabric ghosts. A glass of forgotten water sits on the table next to the bench, probably from earlier in the day when she was waiting for me to come back, and I can't help but picture her sitting here humming along with whatever songs she's been playing. Shae lets go of my hand and perches herself on the piano bench, back to the keys.

"I have an idea," she says as I sit on the coffee table and unzip my guitar case. "What if we both play something we didn't write, just to shake off the nerves a bit. Save the soul-baring part of the evening for full dark?"

The tightness in my chest loosens a little. "Good idea." I throw the guitar strap over my head and start checking the strings for tuning. Without missing a beat, Shae spins on the bench and plays a chord, all the notes I need to check in one harmonious stack. My D string is a little flat, so I tighten the peg until it comes back into balance with the others.

"What should I play first?"

"Is this a bad time to admit that I don't really know what's popular right now?" Shae replies with a laugh. "What about something your band plays on tour?"

After a moment of thought I settle on one and strum a couple of chords to get the feel of playing back into my fingers. Out of the corner of my eye I see Shae's lips twitch with a smile, and my heart thumps hard in my chest right where I've got the guitar pressed against it.

> *Late night, all alone*
>
> *I've had more than a few.*
>
> *Bright light, long gone*
>
> *All I think about is you.*
>
> *Making mistakes is the name of the game,*
>
> *A game I've always played too well.*
>
> *You couldn't live your life that way,*
>
> *Tell me that's why you can't stay.*
>
> *Is this my new reality,*
>
> *Wanting what we'll never be?*
>
> *What we'll never be.*

Shae listens quietly with her eyes closed, taking in the music without distraction. Her eyes open when I finish, and she smiles. "Is that one of yours?"

"No, it's Gabe's actually. He doesn't write a lot of songs, but when he does, they're usually pretty good." And it's easier to sing his words about a girl from his past rather than the ones I've written about a girl in my present...possibly my future. "All right, your turn," I say, slipping the guitar strap back over my head.

Her smile slips a little, replaced by nervousness. "What do you want to hear?"

"Something you're playing for Tampa. One of those things you were telling me about on the beach the other day, the Impressionists."

"All right." She pushes her hair behind her shoulders so it hangs in cascading waves down her back and swivels to face the piano's keyboard again. Her fingers hover over the delicate white keys but she doesn't play. I wait, shifting off the coffee table to sit on the softer sofa underneath a picture of boats that hangs on the whitewashed walls.

Finally, she lowers her hands and begins to play. Soft waves of music roll from the instrument like water in the gulf, flowing and smooth. How can she make it sound so...effortless? My new angle gives me a better view of her fingers as they move over the keys, and I'm stunned at how much control, how much accuracy there is to her movements when it seems like she's barely touching anything at all. Gabe plays keyboards, but where he pounds and crashes, Shae glides and twirls.

I do what she did earlier and close my eyes, leaning back a bit into the sofa cushions so that the music can wash over me. She was right to call it impression music. My imagination is flooding with images... Clouds drifting along in a sunrise sky, tiny waves rippling over the surface of a deep lake, a calm sea...fish swimming lazily along the bottom of a shallow pool, a waterfall rushing over a rocky ledge under the moonlight. But my favorite image is one of Shae herself, long hair rippling in the wind, a perfect embodiment of the music she loves.

"So...what do you think?"

I shake myself back to reality and find Shae has stopped playing and is watching me with apprehension in her face. "I think I've never heard anything like it before and wasn't prepared for how it would make me feel. Was that... Debussy?" I'm sure I butchered the pronunciation, but it's the only name I can remember of the ones she mentioned earlier.

"Liszt this time. His 'Impromptu Nocturne.' It's one of the pieces I used for my audition at Tampa."

"No wonder they said yes. It was..." But I don't have words to describe what it makes me think of because it's new and different. Like Shae. "It was like experiencing a piece of you."

Even in the dark I can tell she's blushing by the way her gaze lowers and she rubs her fingers along the polished wood of the piano bench. "Maybe I should plow through and play the song I wrote before I get nervous again." She hesitates and then peeks up at me through her long, dark lashes, face shadowed by the patchy light coming through the window. "Promise you won't judge me?" Her big eyes are serious, almost begging for confirmation that I'm going to extend my love to whatever song she plays.

"I promise." And it's true, I do.

She turns back around to the piano in the dark, the ivories lit only by the streetlights, and the darkness adds to the mystery of her skill. She plays from memory, from instinct, a soul and its music fusing together in the night.

The song she plays is long and complicated, and though it isn't like the Liszt thing she played before, I like it even more. Each piece fits perfectly with the others together, sweeping melody and supporting harmony, and I find myself leaning forward on the sofa instead of relaxing back, eager for more, my blood zipping through my veins with a strange energy. This isn't music from the soul of a long-dead composer. This is the song of Shae's heart, and—somehow—I know it.

When Shae hits the final notes, the tones hum in the empty night for a moment before they disappear into nothing. She doesn't turn around to face me, but rather stares down at the piano in the half-light, almost as if she's embarrassed or worried that if she turns around, I'm going to be judging her.

And maybe I'm judging her a little bit, but it's not the way she thinks. I'm judging her because she's probably the most wonderful person I've ever met, and I'm completely falling head over heels for her.

"You're amazing." My voice is low and a little ragged because I'm somehow out of breath.

I can see even from this distance that Shae's face turns red again with the compliment.

"You don't have to say that, you know. I can take constructive criticism."

"Shae, seriously. That was brilliant. Beautiful. I loved it."

She tries hard to hide the smile cracking across her face but doesn't do well because it peeks over her cheekbones before completely taking over. "Your turn?"

I suck in a breath, suddenly nervous because I can't possibly follow with my silly song after what she's given me. "Mine isn't anything like yours. There isn't even an ending, it's just...incomplete."

"Maybe I can help you finish it? I'm not great with lyrics but I can always try. Two heads are better than one in times like this."

"Okay. But same rules for you, you're not allowed to judge me."

"Noted."

My guitar is leaning against the sofa next to me where I put it when Shae played the Liszt. It's an old acoustic that my dad gave me on my twelfth birthday, six months before he died of lung cancer. The moment I get the instrument in my hands, I feel transformed and more confident, like I could take on every audience, every waterfront in the entire state—hell, the whole world—with Shae watching me. She's still perched on the piano bench, the now-rising moon reflecting off her hair, making lines on the floor that reach my feet next to the coffee table.

Strumming a few chords, I let myself play through part of the song before I introduce my singing voice, low and quiet.

> *The eyes are crystals; the air's nothing but a breeze*
>
> *I'm in the passenger's seat and someone else has the keys*

I fit a few more chords in after the first verse, flicking my eyes up to Shae so fast I hope she doesn't notice. When I look at her, she has her head tilted to the side, listening.

> *The blue's in front of us with the dark gray behind*
>
> *I'm tangled and twisted up and my soul's so unkind*

It's around the chorus when I finally get my tone right, my voice stops wavering, and I feel like she might actually be enjoying the song enough for me to put my heart into it.

> *But she's there and she's barely breathing*
>
> *I'm here and my heart is bleeding*
>
> *And I push through the three-in-the-morning thoughts*
>
> *And I push through all the three-in-the-morning thoughts*
>
> *As we turn off*
>
> *And we turn on*
>
> *Around the corner of a little place*
>
> *Called Mermaid Avenue*

I strum away at the guitar strings, the song ringing through the house and probably out of the front windows that I totally forgot were open until now. Watching Shae listen to me sing and play gives me a thrill I didn't expect, the same zinging feeling in my veins that I felt when she played her song. The way she sits on the bench, both feet on the floor, hands pressed hard into the wooden top so she can lean in closer makes me think she feels something similar.

> *I wake in the empty morning, the space next to me cold*
>
> *I'm barely awake and I'm chaos and uncontrolled*
>
> *The sunrise is lemonade; but life's nothing but a fray*

My heart's beating but it's distant and astray

The ocean's in front of us with the sandy edge of white

I'm indigo and she's all the stars in the night

But she's there and she's barely breathing

I'm here and my heart is bleeding

And I push through the three-in-the-morning thoughts

And I push through all the three-in-the-morning thoughts

As we turn off

And we turn on

Around the corner of a little place

Called Mermaid Avenue

I play a few more chords, pick at the guitar strings, and try to end the song as best as I can without it sounding too awkward. I don't have anything else to close the song, just the ending of the chorus that doesn't quite feel like the conclusion of the music. But maybe Shae can help me write something. Maybe we'll be able to do this together.

Shae doesn't say anything as I end the song, she just smiles and turns back to the piano, immediately replicating the chords I was playing. She swivels her head back to me, checking to see if it's right, and when I nod, she writes her own line of music—a partial bridge, to tie the whole thing together. And I recognize it. It's part of the melody she just played, the one she wrote before she even heard my song. The back of my neck tingles all the way up my scalp, but I keep playing, pushing forward, and then Shae opens her mouth and sings. Her voice is mellow and soft, something in line with cool jazz or a lounge singer.

> *We collide, the night barely awake, the moon alive in the dark*
>
> *Fingers twisted around one another*
>
> *Bodies like waves*
>
> *Hearts like sirens*
>
> *Souls entwined, we collide*

I strum the guitar strings as Shae continues to play just the right notes, and together we sing the chorus again, with her weaving more of those intricate waves of her own song through my sturdy chords.

> *But she's there and she's barely breathing*
>
> *I'm here and my heart is bleeding*
>
> *And I push through the three-in-the-morning thoughts*
>
> *And I push through all the three-in-the-morning thoughts*
>
> *As we turn off*
>
> *And we turn on*
>
> *Around the corner of a little place*
>
> *Called Mermaid Avenue*

And then in unison, we both pull back to something softer and Shae is the one who ends the song as I strum quietly to accent her voice.

As we turn off

And we turn on

Around the corner of a little place

Called Mermaid Avenue

My heart is beating so hard and fast that it feels like it's going to burst right through my ribcage as the air around us fills with silence once more. I can't process what just happened and I don't want to. All I want is to press Shae against my chest and see if her pulse is as intense as mine, to feel the rhythm of her heart meld into mine the way our minds, our voices, our souls just did.

"Ash?" Her voice is breathy and quiet, like she's having as much trouble breathing as I am.

Very slowly she turns to face me, and I set my guitar down. Still moving in near-perfect unison, we both rise and close the distance until there's barely an inch of space between us. Shae looks up at me and I look down at her, and a moment later, we do as the song we wrote together suggested: we collide, fingers twisted around one another, bodies like waves, hearts like sirens, souls entwined. The only difference between the song and reality is that we're both breathing, lips touching, holding in air to save for the moments when our mouths are pressed together in kisses that last so long we're left gasping. I'm tangled in Shae, and she's wrapped around me, and we're both sinking into a deep and glorious oblivion.

Chapter Ten

SHAE

It takes all my willpower to pull myself away from Asher. Every part of me is screaming that it wants this, wants him, but there's one tiny corner of myself that doubts, and it's like a single pebble disturbing the whole pond with ever-growing ripples. *It's too soon...too quick...you're not ready.*

"Ash," I gasp his name the next time our lips part for air. "Ash, I...I need a moment."

He stops at once, still holding me close but no longer searching for my lips. I can feel the beat of his heart and the heaving of his chest; he's as breathless as I am.

"Too much?" He repeats his question from earlier, but grinning instead of frowning with concern, his forehead resting lightly against mine.

My laugh is shaky with adrenaline and feelings. "Yes and no. It's just going fast again, and I don't know which way is up or down." I lean forward and brush my lips against his softly, so he knows I'm not sorry about what we're doing. "Can we slow down? Just a little?"

"Always." The word is throaty and hoarse, but I know in my soul that he means it because he lets out a comfortable sigh that resonates through my body and all the way down to my toes.

We stand there next to the piano for a little while with our arms around each other. I'm not sure how much time passes because the clock on the adjacent hallway wall ticks into the calmness of the house, making a rhythm with every pulsation of my heart.

"I've never done anything like that before," I whisper into the darkness.

"Me neither. But something about it seemed right. Like all the pieces fit together at just the right time."

I lean back a bit so that I can look into his face. "Is that not what it's like when you write music with Gabe and Chance?"

He shakes his head. "Not like that. When you were playing it felt like...like you'd heard my song before and written your own to match it. But we wrote them before we knew anything about each other. How is that possible?"

A little shiver runs along my spine at his words. "That's exactly what it was like for me too. I saw inside you and—and you could see inside me too. No judgement, no fear of making a mistake or sharing something I didn't want to share. No holding back."

"You hold yourself back?"

"Well, don't you? With Gabe and Chance?"

"Good point," he says with a crooked grin.

A sudden wave of exhaustion rushes over me, and my eyelids grow heavy. Apparently baring your soul to someone is a draining experience. "Any chance we could take this discussion somewhere more comfortable?"

Asher's eyes brighten and then darken again almost at once. "You said you wanted to go slower. I don't want to do anything you're not okay with."

"And that's how I know that bringing you back to my bedroom is a good idea," I reply, pulling out of his arms and instead taking him by the hand, "because you, Asher, are a good person."

In a moment we're under my quilt again, my head cradled between Asher's shoulder and his bicep as he runs his fingers softly through my hair. There's a rumbling in his chest and I realize he's humming his song—*our* song now. My voice isn't as nice as his, but I hum along, too, and he brings his other arm up to wrap me in a warm embrace.

"You're really something else, Shaeline Samson."

"So are you, Asher...whatever your last name is." I don't know his last name. I've made out with him *how* many times in the last two days and not *once* did I even think to ask such a simple question! It's a good thing it's so dark he can't see me blushing, though he can probably feel the heat of my cheeks right through his thin shirt.

"It's Lohan. Asher Lohan."

"You're kidding? Like the actress?"

"Yup. But no relation."

"Poor boy. I was going to say, if you were related, you're missing a golden opportunity to cash in on that connection for your band." I mean it as a joke and hope he can hear it in my voice.

Apparently, he does because his chest shakes with a light chuckle and he half-sings, "I'm just a poor boy, I need no sympathy."

"'Bohemian Rhapsody,' right?"

"Hey, look at you! Knowing something popular for once." He jerks away before I can jab him in the ribs. "I learned to watch out for those fingers of yours this morning. You won't catch me off guard again."

Then the hand he has draped over my arm slides down and he tickles my side. I shriek and try to wiggle away, but I'm too well wrapped in his arms. The sheets twist around our legs as I squirm, but Asher stops before it gets to be too much, instead staring into my eyes and resting his palm flat against my hip.

"Can I kiss you?" he asks, his voice gentle and completely devoid of wheedling or pressuring or any of the tones Evan used to use.

"Yes."

His fingers find mine and we link them together, sitting in the light of the moon as the scent of jasmine and the beach surrounds us. I think—no, I know—I'm in love. It's this moment here, combined with the music and the lyrics and the way I feel when he touches me, that tells me so.

"I have a question for you. And I'm not sure how you're going to take it, and it might potentially ruin everything, but all I know is I have to ask it because I don't want to leave you in a few days."

"Okay. Ask." I rub my thumb against the top of his hand, drawing lines that make up some unknown illustration.

He breathes deeply before slowly letting the words out. "Will you come on tour with me and the guys for the summer?"

The air gets sucked out of the room like a vacuum and suddenly I can't breathe. I want to tell him that of course I will, but instead I pretend I'm rolling his words around in my head and probably my heart, trying to figure out what exactly he's asking and if it's too much. To be honest, I can't help but wonder if he's doing the same thing, trying to ascertain if he should take the words back and pretend they never happened; rewind the night back to a minute ago when he hadn't just potentially ruined it all.

I adjust myself on the bed, still holding Asher's hand but turning to face him in the indigo. "Are you sure that's a good idea?"

"I'm more sure about it than I've ever been about anything else." His words sound certain, but his tone says otherwise, and I call him out on it.

"You're scared of this, aren't you?"

He nods. "A little. It's overwhelming. I mean that in a good way, but I don't know what else to do to keep from leaving you. I can't just go to Tampa for the waterfront night shows knowing that you're here alone for the summer."

"What if I start with coming to Tampa? I can check out the school and the city. It's only, what, a week-long thing?"

"Ten days," he clarifies.

"Ten days in Tampa. I can handle that as a major commitment with some stranger." She grins, squeezing my hand.

"Are you serious?"

I bob my head. "I'm serious. I'll come to the Tampa Buskers Festival with you. I mean, I have no job, no boyfriend, and no best friend left here in Emerald Beach. Mom's not here to tell me what to do. I have this last free summer at my fingertips, and I want to use it. Maybe you can even let me play keyboards some nights when Gabe's off perusing for someone to spend the night with."

My heart pounds a tympanic rhythm in my ribs as I think about playing music with Asher on the waterfronts in the dark under moonlight.

"I'd love that. I'd absolutely love it. I just—shit, I can't believe you said yes."

"You've been worried for a while about that, hmmm?"

"It's crossed my mind a few times." He drops his voice a level, the tone barely above a whisper as I tilt my head against his and touch his forehead with mine.

★

"Hey, Ash, I think I figured out what was wrong with that bridge we were trying to write earlier."

Asher comes in from the kitchen. He's got Mom's Kiss the Cook apron on over his T-shirt and board shorts and a sauce-covered spoon in one hand. "Let's hear it."

I play an E Major chord progression. "We were trying to pivot on this chord," I say, playing it and then changing keys, "right where you sing *don't wanna forget this feeling*, but really the pivot should happen here at *the tide's rising*." My fingers move over the keys, playing the new version with the key change further into the bridge.

"That's it!" Asher says, bobbing his head enthusiastically. "Where were you when I was stuck on about ten different songs and didn't write anything for a year?" He leans down and brushes a kiss against my cheek, and I turn quick to catch him on the lips instead.

We're getting better at these little casual signs of affection, figuring out ways to signal each other with what we want. I was nervous when I first told Asher that a light peck on the cheek would make me feel more like kissing him than starting straight in with the lips, but he took to it at once and never seems to expect anything in return. In fact, I like surprising him with a full kiss now because he really *doesn't* see it coming, even after five days of being together.

And when I'm feeling in the mood to initiate a kiss, I run my fingers along the back of his neck and do my best to make sure he knows I don't expect him to do anything more than enjoy it if that's what he needs.

"Spaghetti's ready," he says when we break apart. "If you come now, the garlic bread will still be edible."

"Oh!" I squeal and jump off the piano bench. "I forgot!" It was my job to make the garlic bread, but it completely slipped my mind after I put it in the oven and sat back down to work on our latest song. "Why didn't you tell me the timer went off?" Asher follows me into the kitchen where I find the tray of garlic bread, unevenly sliced but looking perfectly golden and crispy next to a salad and a pot of spaghetti. "You jerk!" I say, rounding on him, but I'm not actually angry and he's grinning and looking proud of himself.

"How else was I supposed to pull you away from that piano? Creative genius needs to eat sometimes too." He pulls a plate over to the pasta pot and scoops out a hearty helping.

"You know, some famous composers had the weirdest quirks when it came to food," I say, accepting the plate and adding some salad on the side. "Erik Satie claimed he only ate things that were the color white, and Beethoven would only drink coffee that had been made with exactly sixty beans."

"How do you get away with eating only white-colored foods?" Asher asks as he takes a seat next to me at the counter. "What even is just white? Coconuts?"

"Some seafood is pretty pale... Chicken, I guess. Most animal fat."

Asher screws up his face in disgust. "Gross. No thanks."

After dinner, we wash the dishes quickly and race each other back to the living room for another round of songwriting. The one I was working on before dinner is sitting propped on my music stand, scribbled out on a series of staff paper sheets. There are four more on the coffee table, all the product of staying up late, reading each other's musical cues and finding the rhythm of our hearts in the words.

"Think Evan will finally give up and not try to come see you tomorrow?" Asher asks as he picks out some fingering on his guitar.

"He hasn't gotten the hint yet."

"Damn, another day on the beach avoiding your ex-boyfriend and watching your hair flow in the salt breeze. What a bummer." Asher's dark-blue eyes twinkle at me from across the room. He plays a little riff he's been toying with all day and then digs into his pocket and pulls out his phone. "Text from Gabe," he says, swiping the screen with one thumb. "Probably wondering if I'm ever going to sleep at the condo again."

"Doubtful. You've only got a couple more nights before you head off to Tampa for the festival." Even saying it makes the air in the room feel heavier. We've been purposefully avoiding talking about Asher's impending departure. I don't know what his band plans to do when the Buskers Festival ends, but Gabe and Chance are probably getting tired of eating at the same four restaurants every night and striking out with all the girls in town because everyone's been paired up since junior high. As for Asher...sometimes I think he's on the verge of saying *something*, but neither of us tries very hard to get it out of him.

Maybe it's better that we just keep pretending he isn't leaving.

"Gabe wants to know if we're up for meeting at Tin Fish tonight. I told him we've already eaten."

I play a couple of gloomy minor chords in a staccato pattern. "I feel bad for keeping you away from your friends so much."

"Don't. I'd much rather be here with you."

When I keep playing sad notes and don't reply, Asher sets his guitar down and comes to sit next to me on the bench.

"Hey, are you all right?"

"What are we doing, Ash?" I say with a sigh. My fingers move instinctively over the piano keys, combining the random notes into a melancholy tune.

His eyes flick down to watch me play. "Writing a breakup song, apparently." It could be a joke, but I can hear sadness behind the light tone of his voice.

"At some point we have to talk about what happens when you leave."

"I've been hoping someone would figure out how to stop time before then."

That does make me laugh a little, enough to stop needing the release playing out my feelings on the piano provides. I twist and bring one knee up to rest on the bench between us. When I hold out my hand, Asher automatically twines his fingers around mine.

"There was something I wanted to do tonight," he finally says. A muscle twitches in his arm, sending a ripple through his sleeve tattoo. "But you don't have to do it if it makes you nervous."

My stomach does a cartwheel, and twenty different possibilities shoot through my imagination in quick succession. "What did you have in mind?"

Asher reaches back into his pocket and pulls out his phone again. "I thought maybe we could record the songs we wrote. Writing them down is good, but it doesn't capture the feeling we get when we're playing and singing together. Then...whatever happens, we'll always have a little piece of each other."

It's not what I was expecting. Actually, it's almost sadder than him saying he thinks we should part ways tonight and never speak to each other again. Carrying around a little piece of Asher might have been enough for me two days ago, but now...now I'm not sure.

"No pressure or anything," he adds quickly, and I realize I've just been sitting here staring at him.

"It's a lovely idea," I say and squeeze his hand for good measure. If Tampa doesn't work out and we are going to be saying goodbye, I'd rather have a little of him than none at all.

Asher gets up and shuffles through our song notes. "Which one should we do first?"

I should probably choose the one he wrote for me after our first meeting, but there's always a particularly strong surge of emotion and energy when we play that one and I don't think I'll be able to handle it, not with how I'm feeling right now. "Let's do *How It Feels*. I want to try my idea for the bridge again."

We set his phone up on the windowsill where hopefully my piano won't drown out his acoustic guitar but the tiny microphone will still be able to pick up both of our voices. Asher stands behind me so that he can read the music over my shoulder. It's a cobbled-together mess of penciled melody notes and stacked chords with their guitar notations over the top. The first notes are Asher's and he counts out the beat softly before starting in on his riff. This is probably the most up-tempo song we've written: his fingers practically fly along the fingerboard.

> *Give me a day like the one we just had*
>
> *The sun and the waves, pockets full of sand,*
>
> *My heart floats away on a jasmine-kissed breeze,*
>
> *Follow wherever you lead.*
>
> *Make my heart race, try to keep pace,*
>
> *Learn something new with each smile on your*

face

Don't wanna forget how it feels to be here with you now,

The tide's rising up and we'll never come down.

Racing you, chasing you all along the shore,

Love you forever, forever and more...and more... and more...

I can't help it. My mood is already lifting as the song progresses. The piano accompaniment I wrote fades in slowly through the first verse, which Asher sings alone, until it's fully present for the chorus. The lyrics are all his, and I grin as I remember rolling out of bed at three in the morning to find him feverishly scribbling them down on a notebook he pulled off my computer desk. He wrote the first verse about me, and probably would have written the rest like that, too, if I hadn't insisted that at least some of the lyrics be about him.

Dark eyes as blue as the depths of the sea,

Still getting used to your feelings for me.

One thing's for certain, I like how it feels,

Thinking this might be for real.

Make my heart race, try to keep pace,

Learn something new with each smile on your face

Don't wanna forget how it feels to be here with you now,

The tide's rising up and we'll never come down.

Racing you, chasing you all along the shore,

Love you forever, forever and more...and more... and more...

Asher joins me for the chorus, taking a harmony line to my melody, and then we're at the bridge. My fingers take over the chordal structure while Asher returns to his earlier riff, and he improvises a couple of new licks as he leads into the repeat of the lyrics. Right at the moment I pointed out earlier, we both remember the key change and pivot together into the new key. It's still a comfortable range for Asher's voice, but only on the melody, so I take over with a higher harmony.

Don't wanna forget how it feels to be here with you now,

The tide's rising up and we'll never come down.

Racing you, chasing you all along the shore,

Love you forever, forever and more...and more... and more...

Asher signals for me to sit quiet for a ten-count after we finish the song, leaving a little bit of dead space at the end of the recording. Then he reaches out and picks up his phone and presses the "stop" button on the screen.

"Please tell me you felt that like I did."

His eyes are glowing with excitement as he grips my hand again. I can practically feel the energy sizzling on his skin when I touch him, and my lips split into a grin despite the little knot of cold that still burrows in my chest. "I think that was our best one yet."

"Your fix to the bridge was perfect. I just wish I had my electric with me. That solo in the middle would be more powerful if I had a little more power to work with. Actually—" he pauses for a moment, considering. "Would you mind if I ran back to the condo and brought over my electric and an amp? I promise I'll keep the noise down for the neighbors."

"Sure. Do you want to borrow my mom's car? It'll be easier than lugging everything over on foot."

"Good idea. You drive and I'll run in and grab my stuff."

I shake my head, thinking fast. "No, actually, I think it might be better if I stay here. Mom texted earlier saying she might call. If I call her instead, she'll be less likely to interrupt us." And I'll have a few minutes where I don't have to hide my disappointment over Asher's eventual departure.

The keys to Mom's car haven't left the little basket she keeps them in on the hall table since the day before she left. It's not a long walk to any of my usual haunts in Emerald Beach, and frankly the idea of going anywhere around town is laughably boring since I gained the option of staying inside and writing songs with Asher instead.

"Be back soon," he says, taking the keys and squeezing my hand. "Want anything while I'm out?"

"Just hurry back." *We haven't got much time left.*

Chapter Eleven

SHAE

Over the course of the next couple of days, Asher's sunburn starts to fade and our attachment grows deeper. We spend days at the beach on the hot sand, and evenings on the back patio drinking iced teas until the sun goes down. At night once it gets dark, we play music for each other, writing song after song after song about the summer and the crystal waters and everything that's happened throughout the course of finding both at our feet.

The night before we're to leave for Tampa, I'm packing up a long-forgotten suitcase I found in the back of my closet while Asher's on my bed with his guitar, picking away at the strings. The song he's playing sounds familiar in melody only, maybe something from the radio that I heard in passing when I was driving somewhere with the music turned down low. Biting his lip, Asher looks so serious when he concentrates, his fingers plucking at the acoustic notes while I shove clothes and bathing suits from my dresser drawers into the red carry-on.

I must fold and unfold and fold again the same shirt fifty times if I do it once while watching him think.

Eventually, his concentration is broken by something, or he just happens to notice that I've stopped packing.

"What's up?" he asks, placing his hand flat over the strings of the guitar to make a *thrum* noise.

"Just watching the gears turn in your head," I laugh, dropping the pop-over sweater into the suitcase on top of a yellow palm leaf patterned bikini. "It's fascinating to watch you work."

Asher smiles into the darkness of my bedroom, the corner lamp the only thing lighting up the space. I have the dial turned down low for mood more than anything else, probably making it harder on myself to see what exactly I'm packing and if there's anything in the carry-on to match it. It doesn't matter to me, though, because I like the atmosphere.

He rises from the bed and sets the guitar down on the chair in the opposite corner of my room before returning to the mussed-up blankets. "You almost done?"

"Yeah." I toss one final shirt on top of the pile and zip the suitcase closed. "All that's left is a little makeup, my toothbrush, stuff like that. Stuff I'll need in the morning before we leave."

He nods, patting the space on the bed next to him. I pull the suitcase off the quilt and set it down on the floor before crawling over the white sheets. I wrap my fingers in between his calloused ones, my skin dark and tanned against his pale arms. It reminds me a little of Mom and Dad before Dad left—when they would walk along the beach when I was little, I remember seeing their hands joined together in the same way mine and Asher's are now.

Stifling a yawn, I bury myself against Asher's side.

"Tired?" he asks, reaching a hand up to brush a ticklish strand of my hair off his arm.

"A little. Not too much. Just enough to want to lay here for the rest of the night and do nothing."

"No music tonight?"

"Maybe not. I think I'm fresh out of lyrics. You can always play for me, though, if you want. I like to listen to you and the guitar."

"It's all the way over there," Asher replies, giving a nod across the room. "Just like the lamp is all the way over there and I'd like to turn it off."

I sigh, stretching out my toes with a chuckle, before I silently get up and turn off the lamp. Once I do, we're encompassed in darkness, and it takes me a second to find my way back to the bed by the low moonlight cascading through the far window. When I do, Asher's flat on the mattress, and for a second, I think he might have fallen asleep until I start to fumble my way under the blankets in my tank top and knit shorts. He reaches over, rolling onto his side, and wraps an arm around me.

"I've been thinking," he says, his voice low. "But I don't know how you're going to feel about what I have to say."

"You asked me to come to Tampa on tour with you and this is the thing you're not sure about?" I chuckle, shifting over on my shoulder to face Asher.

"Good point. I guess, I was just going to say that, honestly, okay. This is going to sound stupid but sleeping in my shorts has kind of gotten past the point of being comfortable. Especially since we were at the beach today and

I think my pockets are filled with sand. I'm making my own beach over here."

"Is this your way of trying to tell me you're hoping I don't mind if you take off your shorts?" I try to put a serious look on my face, but I just can't. The idea of Asher in my bed almost entirely naked is an image I wouldn't erase for the world. It's something I've been trying to picture since the first night he spent in my bed on the other side of the mattress, and I'm practically drooling at the thought of him undressing in front of me now.

"Um, if you don't mind. I think, yeah."

"Go for it."

Asher doesn't need any more confirmation than that. He wiggles his way out from underneath the quilt and pushes it back along the bed to wipe off the fitted sheet with one hand. I swear I can practically hear the sand hitting the floor as he brushes it off his side of the mattress. Once the grit is gone, or as gone as I can assume it will ever be, he stands on the side of the bed and twists off his shirt before slowly undoing the button of his shorts and then the zipper. He steps out of the bottom layer of clothing until he's in front of me barefoot in a pair of dark boxer briefs that are tight on his thighs.

My whole stomach tingles at the shadowed sight, and before I know what I'm saying or doing, I throw myself over to Asher, grab him by the waist, and pull him down to me on the bed in a deep and heavy kiss. Our lips crash into one another like they did the day by the front door, and it's then I know something inside us has changed. Asher kneels on the bed, shifting me downward so I'm between his knees, with one hand on my stomach and the other on my neck. I can't help the groan that escapes me because everything about the way Asher's touching me feels so good.

"Shae, do you want this?"

"You?" I wrinkle my brow together, keeping my voice barely above a whisper. Considering his question for all of half a second, I reply. "Of course, I want you. I've wanted you since the first day we met."

"I mean it, Shaeline." He pulls away from our embrace and looks down at me with a gaze that's firm but gentle, like the way he says my full name. "Do you want to have sex with me?"

I nod.

"Say yes. I want to hear you say yes." The growl in his voice is prominent, and it sits in my stomach and makes me vibrate down to my toes. I can't stop my legs from shaking, even if I try to think really hard about it.

I finally get the words out, and they're trembling too. "Yes, Asher. Yes."

He smiles, sliding his hand up the underside of my shirt and pulling it swiftly over my head to expose my paisley printed bralette. Sinking into my neck with his lips, he kisses me and murmurs in the middle of his intimate caresses. "I'll be gentle, I promise. And if you get uncomfortable you tell me to stop, okay? We'll only take things as far as you want to go. As far as you're comfortable. And if you're scared or nervous or—"

"Asher?" I brush my fingernail along his shoulder blade and up the back of his neck like I know he enjoys and feel him resist a shiver across his broad back.

"Hmmm?"

"I want to know what you're really like. I want to see this part of your soul."

Asher chuckles into my ear, the timbre quiet. I respond by thumbing the back of his hair, wrapping my fingers around it, and giving a little tug, smirking. "Maybe next time, Shae. The first time isn't the time for that. Don't tempt me. And just promise me you'll tell me if—"

"I'll tell you to stop if I want you to stop, Asher. I want this. I want all of you. I want you and the music and the sex and the everything. All of it. Show me it all."

That's all it takes. Those words, that confirmation. As if pulled in by the moon and the stars and everything around us, Asher's a rogue wave; he collides into me, and I crash right back.

Some time later, I don't know how long, I still haven't stopped shaking, but it's a different kind of vibration. It's a feeling I never felt with Evan, and now I know why I was so hesitant to take the step with him: because it wasn't the right time. This time, here with Asher, felt as perfect as I could have imagined it, if I had been imagining it at all. Maybe, in some ways, I'm like he is. Needing that emotional connection with someone in order to want to sleep with them. There's nothing wrong with not, but for me and Evan—I shudder when I think of his name the second time—that just wasn't the case.

I'm bundled up in a cotton sheet, Asher standing at the window, breathing in the cooler night air and looking at the moon across the patio. He's naked except for the boxer briefs, all his tattoos showing at once, and I realize in the moment that's how I like him best. It's natural and attractive and makes my stomach flip-flop in my chest when I gaze over his strong back and thick thighs.

He catches me looking, and a blush creeps up my cheeks that he can't see in the dark.

"Like what you see?" he asks, his voice playful as he crosses the room, passing the end of the bed back to his side of the mattress. Asher doesn't sit, though; instead, he first picks up his acoustic guitar from the chair, and then props himself up against the headboard.

I nod, still somewhat speechless from everything we just experienced together. It's been a perfect week of the summer I didn't expect to have at all. After losing Evan and Livi and my job, Asher's been a saving grace. And this, all this, the music and the experiences and the *whatever this is* have been more than I ever could have imagined would fit into seven days.

He strums a note into the silence, then a chord, then another note. It's something I haven't heard before and immediately I can tell that Asher feels inspired to write something new. The picking of the strings quivers in the soft spot of the back of my neck, causing a shiver that goes both up and down my spine. It's as if I'm feeling the music of the guitar like I felt the piano the first night after I ran into Asher at the Mermaid Avenue sign.

"Something on your mind?" I ask, loosening the sheet around me to allow the air from the open window to blow around my warm body.

"Just a little song. Well, maybe part of a song. Want to hear?"

"Of course."

Asher starts the strumming over again, replaying the beginning of what he just wrote before he starts to sing.

Underneath a summer sunset

Can't hold on but can't let go

We're going down and you can feel it and so can I

Slow dancing under drunk skies and iced tea nights

Every one of them a feeling

Every one of us a feeling

Of pretty girls and pretty words

And pretty sunrises

All the pretty things in a life

Asher pauses then, looking up at me with a tender grin. "It doesn't have a chorus. It needs to have a chorus."

"Says who? The king of music writing? I like it as it is. You're just singing out your feelings. I think there's something special about that. It doesn't have to be cyclical or follow a structure in improvisation. It can be whatever you want it to be."

"What would you write about, if you were playing the piano right now?" He leans on the top of the guitar, adjusting his leg underneath himself.

Thinking for a second, I bite the inside of my cheek and adjust the sheet again for the second time so it doesn't totally display my bare chest. Not that I'm sure what I'm hiding, because Asher got enough of a look at my body that there's nothing left to keep concealed. "I'd play something quiet, maybe in a minor key. Something with a lot of low notes that make you feel like you're in the dark but something's happening. Something important and intimate and special."

"I like that."

Asher hums to himself for a few more minutes before he looks back at me. I quirk the corner of my lip up. "I'd play something for you but I'm much too comfortable to get up and go out to the living room. Plus, I'd have to get dressed."

He laughs, setting the guitar back down on the chair next to the bed. "Says who?"

I swat at his arm lightheartedly, the sound of skin on skin making a little *thwak* noise. He pretends I've hurt him, rubbing at his arm with dramatics, but the smile on his face tells me that it didn't injure him in the least.

We spend the rest of the night in bed, talking and laughing and being with each other, quietly observing the silence of the house as Asher slowly drifts off to sleep. I watch him breathe for a moment, not able to believe the magnitude of everything we've just done. Eventually, at some point in the wee hours of the morning, my legs stop their intermittent shaking, my breathing slows, and I sink into the pillows as well. Once my head finds a comfortable spot on the cool gel of the memory foam, I allow the night to take me away into a dreamless slumber that's the deepest I've slept in what feels like forever.

Chapter Twelve

ASHER

I dream about Shae, just like I have for the last week. We're on the beach, on the boardwalk, on Mermaid Avenue, playing music in Tampa, and everywhere in between. That's half the reason I'm not surprised when I wake up and she's stuffing some more things into her suitcase, trying to smush the thing closed with it already overflowing with everything she could possibly think she needs for ten days on the road. I haven't logistically figured out how we're going to fit an extra bag and person in the minivan with all our instruments and ourselves, but we've made it fit before when Chance was seeing that girl in Orlando so we can make it work for Shae.

The morning is quiet, and we tinker around on our respective instruments and eat granola bars for breakfast before Gabe finally pulls up in front of the house.

"You ready?" I pick up my guitar case and gym bag and hoist it over my shoulder. I've always traveled pretty light, but the summer weather means less fabric and less space taken up in my bag for things like sweaters.

She looks a little nervous, biting her lip as she pulls out the handle of her suitcase. "Yeah. I'm ready."

"Did you text your mom this morning to let her know you were going on tour with a stranger you only met last week?"

The joke seemingly breaks up her worry and dissolves it into the hot Florida air. A smile breaks across her face and she swats me out of the front door so she can leave last and lock up. While I carry our things to the black minivan in the previously empty driveway, Gabe pops open the trunk for me to shove whatever I can inside. I manage to find a spot for Shae's suitcase, but my guitar and duffel will have to go in the back seat, meaning that Shae and I will be squashed together for the drive to Tampa. I'm not complaining.

We crawl into our seats, shuffling around my belongings until we're as comfortable as we're going to get sitting with a guitar practically in our laps. Thankfully, Emerald Beach is close enough to Tampa—and home in Genesis Lake—that we have the luxury of trucking our electronics around each day to the Buskers Festival. Which reminds me, all of a sudden, that Shae's going to see the condo I may or may not have left as an absolutely perfect disaster when the guys and I passed through from Orlando on our way to Emerald Beach.

To be fair, I've never had to worry about anyone coming in and surprising me other than Gabe and Chance, and their place is even worse than mine.

"Hi, lovebirds." Chance twists around in his seat as Gabe pulls out of the driveway. "Nice to see you two have unwrapped yourselves from each other long enough to join us on tour."

Shae chuckles, shifting her position on the bench seat. I never know how she's going to take Chance's comments, but her nature seems happy to appreciate him in stride. "I couldn't not come. A summer alone versus a summer with a traveling band? Like that's even a choice."

I find the corners of my lips tipping upward in a little smile, my fingers itching for Shae's, and I lean close and brush her palm until she wraps her hand in mine.

The trip to Tampa takes close to two hours, driving along the gulf because we have time to spare. The blue of the water is crystalline like in Emerald Beach, but for whatever reason it doesn't seem to have the same shine as it did the day I met Shae or the night we had dinner at Tin Fish. Gabe and Chance chatter in the front of the van while Shae and I look out of the backseat windows, watching as the world goes by. She draws little pictures on my palm as Gabe weaves the vehicle through the streets, right to the edge of town where Genesis Lake starts before you get into the Tampa city limits. I like where I live, flowers everywhere and blue sky matching the water, like the world is infinite in the cerulean glow.

"I didn't tell you much about my place," I say to Shae as she traces another line on my hand. Little shoots of electricity run up my arm and I really want to kiss her, but I can't because we're in a moving vehicle and there's two guys in the front who might not appreciate the public display of affection. "I feel like maybe I should have in one of our million conversations."

"I'm sure it's wonderful. I'm not worried." She shrugs, poking at the middle of my hand gently to accentuate her point.

"It's a little messy, I didn't expect to have guests pretty much, well, ever."

"Like I said," she repeats, only a slight waver in her voice. "I'm sure it's great."

I hadn't really stopped to think about what she would do if it wasn't great, if she desperately wanted to go back home, if she hadn't planned on staying in my own personal bubble for the ten days we're here outside Tampa. Maybe I should have. Maybe things didn't seem so complicated until now. And suddenly, for the first time in what feels like a long time, I start to worry.

Gabe stops in front of my building, which is only two streets over from where he and Chance live, a yellow stucco new construction that I can only afford because of the money Dad left me when he passed. Like I always do when I see the sign out front for The Sagewood Condominiums, I say a little thanks to Dad and nod toward the clouds.

"Pick you up at six thirty," Gabe notes with his window down as we hoist our things out of the van and onto the circular front drive of the building. Only a minute later, guitar in my hand and bags at our feet, Shae and I are left alone again.

We carry everything up to the seventh floor, and when I open the door to face the long windows of my living room, clothes strewn over the back of my living room chair and couch, Shae smiles politely at the view.

"This is really nice, Ash."

"Thanks. Um, you can bring your things into the bedroom. I'll get it all tidied up for you. I'll sleep out here on the couch so—" I pause, not sure what I'm trying to say. I don't want her to feel pressured for us to sleep together in my bed, even though we've been sleeping in hers for the last number of days. I'm getting tense as I consider the options, holding my breath as I wait for her to respond.

She crinkles her forehead. "You don't have to sleep on the couch. This is your place; I can sleep there if you don't want—"

I know she's thinking now that I don't want to be in the same bed as her, which wasn't my intent at all. Now I feel like an idiot for overthinking the boundaries of whatever is going on between us.

"No, no. I want to. I just thought maybe you'd want some privacy since this is, I don't know, new?"

"What's *this*?" She kicks off her shoes and walks into the living room to sink into a chair, the only one without clothes on the back. I know exactly what she's asking because I've heard girls ask the same question to Gabe and Chance. Somehow, it's different when it's being asked to me.

I prop up my guitar case along the entryway wall, trying to mentally prepare myself for the conversation. "Do you want to define it? Does it need that?"

Shae ponders for a moment and then shakes her head as she tucks her legs underneath herself, getting cozy in the chair. "I don't think so. I think it just is what it is. I'm fine with it just existing."

An audible breath of air is released back into the room, and Shae's corresponding laugh loosens me back up.

"You were worried we were getting into something serious, weren't you?" She tilts her head to the side, sunlight streaming over her dark hair and making it appear more violet and crimson.

I shake my head, trying to seem confident about the action. "Not really, I mean, if it's a conversation we need to have, then it's a conversation we need to have. But maybe we should have had it before we got here for ten days."

"I think we're good. I'm good, I mean. Are you good?"

"I'm fine."

Shae gives me a crooked smile, but I can see she's picking at the edge of her thumb. To me that means everything isn't good, that she's nervous about something, but maybe she just feels awkward here in my place.

"I'm thinking a drink would be good." My voice sounds awkward and pressed, probably because I don't know what to do with a girl in my condo. Maybe Shae felt like this with me in her house, or maybe worse since I was a total stranger. "I'm not sure I have much other than Vitamin Water and cans of soda. Preference?"

"I'll take a water."

I escape into the kitchen and consider banging my head against the wall for being so clumsy and weird about this whole thing. Instead, I dig through the fridge for two lemonade Vitamin Waters behind all the takeout boxes and containers of yogurt. When I locate them, I stand with my back against the cool stainless steel for a moment, feeling the chill across my back. I can't help myself when I have a million thoughts running through my head all at the same time. Did we make a mistake? Why does this suddenly feel so abrupt? Am I just terrified of what comes next?

When I look up a moment later, Shae's silently standing in the doorway, leaning against the wall.

"Everything okay?" I break out of my trance and hand over the water to her. She twists off the cap and takes a sip before responding.

"I could ask you the same thing."

I let out a little puff of air and smile. Now isn't the time to start lying so I might as well be honest. At least if this is the start of things totally falling apart, then I still have time to drive Shae back home before we get too uncomfortable.

"Asher?"

"Yeah, sorry. Just thinking. I guess this is all pretty new to me and I'm overthinking everything. I've never had a girl live with me even overnight, let alone for ten days. It's just something that hit me all of a sudden and I think I'm worried and overly, I don't know, self-conscious?"

Shae nods, taking another drink from the plastic bottle. "I'm scared, too, Ash. You can just say you're scared. It's overwhelming and fast and I don't think it really hit me until I walked through your door that this could be real."

"It's real, Shae. Everything I feel is real."

There's a pause between us then, as Shae fiddles with the plastic ring around the bottle lid. She twirls it around and around a few times before she finally speaks.

"Everything I feel is real too. I never felt this way with Evan. I've only felt this way with you. It started the moment I saw you, it happened when we were on the beach, and in bed, and everywhere else. It's the universe telling us something."

When she says it like that, it sounds so beautiful and honest. And I love it. I love her words and I love the way she says them and the way she translates her thoughts into music for my ears. And on top of it all, I know right in the moment she says that the galaxy is speaking to us that I love her too. It's all through my body from my fingers to my toes.

"Shae?" I say her name as she has the Vitamin Water to her mouth, and her gaze flicks up to me while she sips. I place my unopened drink on the counter; my breath hitches in my throat for a second before I throw the words out into the afternoon air. "I'm in love with you."

The statement explodes into the open concept condo, reverberating off the sand-colored walls, causing my heart to pound hard and my vision to get a little blurry around the edges. There's a sensation in the pit of my stomach that I can't identify, something like sickness and nervousness all mixed together, and it makes me think maybe I'll pass out. Based on Shae's reaction, for a second, I think that maybe I only said the words in my head, and she didn't hear me. However, when I go to open my mouth to repeat myself, she sets her opened bottle down on the counter and crosses through the galley kitchen to fall headlong into my lips, toppling me against the fridge for balance.

The kiss is singular, but long—long enough that when we break apart, I suck in a hard breath to fill my lungs because I've been entirely depleted of oxygen. We don't move far from each other, my hands still wrapped around Shae's waist and the hem of her shirt, while her arms rest on my shoulders. She smells a little like mint and sea salt, a combination I'm growing fond as hell of.

"I'm in love with you, too, Asher," she whispers, her tone so quiet I can hardly hear it over the sound of the condo air conditioning. It doesn't matter to me how loud she says it, because she's said it. We've said it to each other. We're in love.

"Do you think—" I start to say, but the look in Shae's eyes cuts me off.

"If you're going to ask if it's too fast and too strange then yes, and no. And maybe. But isn't that what makes this wonderful?"

Her words crawl into my brain and make me feel things I didn't know I could feel all at the same time. Contentedness, admiration, compassion, desire. Absently, I look over at the clock on the oven to see what time it is, because my mind is going everywhere, and I think I need her. By think, I mean know. I need Shae. And based on the way she's raking her fingers through the back of my hair in the exact way that I like, she needs me too. We need something physical to represent what we've just said.

"Come on." I slide my hands up her arms and gently tug her hands from their spot, making my skin sizzle for more and fogging up my brain. "Let me show you the bedroom. I have a feeling we'll be spending a lot of time in there."

Shae laughs, and we leave the kitchen with our fingers interlaced, me leading her across the tile.

Chapter Thirteen

SHAE

Asher lets me sleep for the rest of the early evening, but I'm in and out of a draggy rest for a couple of hours before he finally comes back in the bedroom and says he has to leave in a few minutes. The sun is low in the sky and makes everything on the walls have an extra hint of yellow, the water sparkling in the distance out of the window and showing me the same gulf that I can see from home, just from a different angle. I roll over under the turquoise sheets and a stark white duvet, stretching before facing him.

"Can I come with?" I push myself up on the bed, holding the fabric to my chest so as to not expose myself too much. I'm not sure what my brain thinks the big deal is, because Asher's already seen me without clothes on several times, but in the daylight when we're not sleeping together, I guess I feel more comfortable covered.

"Of course. But the Festival doesn't end until ten and then we'll need to pack up and all that. You seemed pretty sleepy after all *that* so I wasn't sure if you'd even want to come."

I tuck the sheet around me tight before running a hand through the tangles of my waves and grinning. "I wouldn't miss it for the world. I can't wait to see you guys—Collide—live."

A broad smile breaks across Asher's face, and I can tell he's pleased. "You remembered our name!"

"Of course, I did. That's not just something another musician forgets."

"All right, well, is fifteen minutes okay? Gabe's going to be here then, and he hates being late for setup."

Fifteen minutes? I need to shower, do something with my hair, figure out where Asher's thrown all my clothes...

"Yeah, no worries," I reply anyway, despite my concerns with the lack of time. A quick rinse off and some dry shampoo should be enough for a night on the waterfront watching the music. I start mentally pulling out clean clothes from my suitcase when I realize that it's not even in the room with me. "Um, Asher?"

He's halfway out of the door to let me get ready, but he turns on his heel. "Yeah?"

"Can you get me my suitcase? I don't exactly have anything handy to wear and I'm not sure walking around with no clothes in front of those big windows—"

"Got it. Be right back."

A moment later, Asher brings in my carry-on and sets it right next to the bed, so I barely even have to get up in order to fetch my clothes from inside. "I'll be in the kitchen writing if you need anything, okay?"

"Sure, thanks."

He gives me a quick little kiss before he walks across the room and heads out into the main living area, leaving me alone behind the half-wall separating the two.

Fourteen and a half minutes later we're heading down to meet Gabe and Chance, and the world around me smells like Tropic Vibes shampoo powder and Asher's soap. There's something soothing about the aroma of him on my skin, like he belongs there and around me forever and for always. Someone once told me that scent triggers memories, and if that's true, the perfume of oranges and black pepper and the beach all mixed together will be the thing to forever call Asher to my mind.

The guys are chatty all the way to Tampa, talking about their playlist and which songs they should perform in what order. I sit quietly in the back seat, stuffed between instruments and cords and Asher, watching the waves of the Gulf roll by as we drive. Thoughts trickle through my mind, about the summer, about where in Europe Livi and Evan must be right now, about losing my job at Beaches N' Cream just because of some stupid rumor. It all feels like it doesn't matter anymore, at least not right now. And as for the job to cover the cost of my books, well, I can worry about that later. For now, I think about the ten days I have here in Tampa and Genesis Lake with Asher and what it means to be in love for real.

Before I know it, we're pulling into a car park, and the guys are filtering out of the vehicle and collecting their instruments and cords and electronics to get ready to set up. Asher lets me carry his guitar which feels like an honor, and we head down the sidewalk a little way before coming to Bishop Street on the water.

Crowds have already started to gather, and the waterfront is busier than Emerald Beach on a good day.

"Our spot is 68B, the Brackley Soundstage." Gabe directs us down the waterfront to a small, staged area, lit up with a single spotlight that glows in the late evening. Cords are taped down along the boards so people traveling through don't trip, and I stand back for a moment and watch them seamlessly get organized. As the seconds tick past, they turn more and more into Collide and become less and less like individual people. They're humming along with one another, getting their music ready, and I'm just standing here with a guitar in a case. It's fascinating how they've tuned into one another.

Asher looks over at me once the stage area is set, turning the light a little bit off center so it hits Gabe's keyboards a bit more than the other end of the stage.

"Wanna test them out? We need to check sound. We'll go stand back in the crowd and you play something."

I look at the people gathered around the Brackley Soundstage, some in clumps and others milling about waiting for the show to start. "You want me to play in front of people?"

Asher shrugs. "Only if you want to. I know how you feel about that kind of thing."

I take a deep breath as he approaches. I hand the guitar over Asher as my heart pounds deep in behind my ribs so hard it almost hurts. My palms feel sweaty as an unknown force pushes me up onto the stage, into the bright, offset light. It shines just out of the way of my eyes and thankfully blocks me from seeing a bit of the crowd. With my legs feeling like jelly, I squint to try to find Asher, who has moved farther back in the group, probably to see how far the sound will travel.

"What do you—" the microphone bursts my voice through, causing me to jump. "What do you want me to play?"

"Play something!" Someone hollers from the crowd, the voice not belonging to any of the familiar boys. I debate yelling back at him that I'm not even supposed to be up here, but I don't. Instead, I poise my shaking fingers over the keyboard and hit a couple of gentle notes. They're too quiet. I turn up the volume louder and try again. Scrunching my eyes, I spot Asher giving me a thumbs-up and I tentatively start to improvise the way I feel, turning it into a song just like I would at home.

Nervy notes start the song, my fingers vibrating on the keyboard keys. I try looking out at the crowd again, but it only makes me more nervous, seeing all the strangers out there stopping to listen to me run the sound check of the instrument. Instead, I close my eyes and picture Asher sitting on the couch next to my piano at home, listening to me play music like we did almost ever since the first day we first met. In only a few seconds, a harmony flows from my heart into my fingertips, pressing note after haunting note of a dark song in a minor key. I'm scared, my music is scared, but I'm also in love. And love, so I've heard, conquers all.

When I hit the final notes of the short song, I finally open my eyes just as scattered applause comes from the crowd. The clapping is punctuated by hoots and cheers from Chance, Gabe, and Asher who have approached the soundstage, smiles on all of them from ear to ear. Chance elbows Asher in the side, the gesture playful, and Asher nearly drops his guitar.

"You didn't tell us she could play like *that*."

"I'm not obligated to tell you everything."

Gabe cocks an eyebrow before coming on stage and flipping off the switch to the microphone so the crowd can't overhear our entire conversation. He looks more surprised than he did the day he spotted me on the board-walk outside of Beaches N' Cream. "You're kind of obli-gated to tell us when you're dating a girl who can play the keyboard better than I can. It's just kind—especially now that I have to go on stage after her performance."

"It wasn't a performance," I reply, chuckling and stepping off the raised platform away from the spotlight. "That was just sound check. I was warming up the crowd. And I'm not sure I'd say we're dating, I mean, I guess that's a conversation—"

I look over at Asher and he stares at me with a silly grin on his face. It tells me everything I need to know right in that moment. He told me he's in love with me when we were standing in the kitchen earlier, and I agreed. Of course, we're dating.

"Anyway," Gabe redirects, looking over at the guys. "Might as well get on with it before we lose the crowd."

He and Chance hop up on stage, adjusting equipment quickly as Asher gives me a quick kiss on the forehead. "That was awesome, Shae. Don't feel like you need to stay around here all night, you might as well walk around and watch some of the other shows if you want. Probably go-ing to get boring listening to our songs over and over again."

"I at least want to stay for the first set. I've never heard Collide play, and I'm looking forward to it."

"I hope you like us."

"I know I will."

Asher finally breaks away and steps onto the sound-stage with his guitar, taking a space at the end of the spotlight beams on the far side. Thankfully, the stage is located in a bit of an alcove and there are garden half-walls all along the edge for people to sit if they don't want to stand for the entire show. I climb on the rocks and find a comfortable spot in the fading daylight, just as Gabe starts to rouse the crowd standing in front of them.

"Hi, everyone! We're Collide and we're so happy to be playing here at home for you all tonight. I'm Gabe, this is Chance, and on guitar is Asher, and the first song we're going to play for you is called 'Broken Glass,' and we'll follow it up with 'Love Letters in the Sand.'"

My heart skips as Asher plays the first chord on his guitar, and then Gabe chimes in on the keyboard, while Chance plays a handheld drum beat in the background that filters in. Soon, Gabe's voice rings out over the top of the music and melody, deep and rocky and unexpected—though I'm not sure what I thought his voice would sound like.

> *Shattered bits of broken memories*
> *Like a mirror that's fallen*
> *We chip away at winter's calling*
> *Fractured lust and bitter warnings*
>
> *Little pieces of sharp nostalgia*
> *Every bit cutting my heart*
> *When we're together and apart*
> *Cruel love and mysterious weather*

The tune is catchy and dark, the beat echoing over the lapping of the waterfront and the footsteps of people walking on the worn boards. A larger crowd begins to gather at the soundstage, but thankfully I'm far enough up on the rocky wall that I can see over everyone's heads and hear the music perfectly. The best part of it all is that I can watch Asher from this angle and see him plucking his guitar, his dark hair reflecting the spotlight. He looks so into the music, and I can't help but wonder if that's how I look when I'm playing piano and get in the right mood.

> *We're playing a song of*
>
> *Fire and flames and love*
>
> *But mostly a melody of*
>
> *Broken glass*
>
> *Where we sound like we're crashing*
>
> *But we're falling slowly*
>
> *Then all at once*
>
> *Like broken glass*

It's around this time that my phone rings, and I fetch the device only to see that my mother is calling. The feeling of my heart missing beats only amplifies as the image and number on the screen pulses. Of course, I can't exactly answer her right now, but I also can't ignore the call, and for a moment I'm frozen in a limbo between being in trouble for leaving the city with a strange boy and worrying my mother about what's going on because I didn't answer the ringing phone.

Finally, the phone makes a little *bloop* noise and her picture stops moving, telling me that she's hung up on the other end. Now I don't have to worry about answering the call with a bunch of music and crowds in the background, but I do have to figure out an excuse about what I was doing so that I couldn't answer the phone and wasn't able to call her back, maybe even for hours.

I jump as my phone makes a different noise, telling me that I have a text.

MOM: *Hi, Shaeline. Where are you at?*

The message pops up on the screen, stays for a few seconds, and then disappears. It's just long enough for my thoughts to filter from thinking of an excuse for not answering the phone to straight cursing.

> *Sharp objects and held on lies*
>
> *Leftovers of us in the sea and tide*
>
> *And we throw away a memory*
>
> *Broken bones and broken glass*

I hesitate to type a generic message back because I'm not sure what to say or what Mom wants. It takes me too long to craft something that almost makes sense, and by that point I've missed the entire end of the song, and the start of 'Love Letters in the Sand.' I hope Asher doesn't look up for me at any of these moments, because I don't want him to think that I'm bored. I'm just, well, now I'm worried and trying not to panic.

SHAE: *Hi, Mom. I'm just out for a little while. Is everything okay?*

MOM: *Sure, everything's okay. I just wanted to make sure you were going to be around when I got back. It looks like I left my house key on the front rack, so I need you to let me in the house.*

Wrinkling my eyebrows together at my phone, I type a message back as quickly as my fingers will go.

SHAE: *What do you mean? I thought you were gone for another few weeks?*

MOM: *Don't sound so disappointed, Shaeline. Things didn't exactly work out between Will and me. I'm on Wi-Fi in the airport right now. I'll be home by midnight, so if you can be home from whatever you're doing with Livi or Evan, that would be helpful to me.*

It strikes me that Mom doesn't have any idea about Livi or Evan going to Europe without me, she doesn't know about the breakup, about the fact that I don't have a job, about running into Asher and falling for him—she doesn't know any of it. And she definitely can't know that I'm currently in Tampa with Collide at the Buskers Festival after I was told not to leave Emerald Beach. I was trusted not to leave Emerald Beach.

SHAE: *No problem. I'll unlock the door.*

MOM: *Thanks, I'll see you tonight.*

For the rest of Collide's first set, I try to regulate my breathing and not go into hysterics. I need to get out of Tampa and back home before midnight, but my ride is performing until ten and all my things are strewn about at

Asher's and definitely not ready for me to pack up quickly and hurry home. Plus, I need time to explain what's going on. By the time the half hour of the show passes, I'm wound up so tight that I think I might explode.

Asher finds me on the rocks, and his beaming smile fades quickly into a look of worry. "Shae, are you okay? Is something wrong?"

"My mom called," I begin to explain, but Asher already knows without me having to use my words.

"Is everything okay?"

I nod. "Kind of. Things didn't work out with her and Will."

Asher bites at his bottom lip, clearly understanding what my lack of description means. "When's she coming home? Tomorrow?"

"Tonight. Midnight. I've got to—I mean, I can't not be there."

He bobs his head, rubbing his jaw with his hand. "I'll get you home. We'll figure it out. Skip a set or something to get back to Genesis Lake and pick up my car."

"I'm sorry." I try my best to breathe as Asher reaches out to touch my arm. There's a little sick feeling in my stomach, almost like I'm going to throw up the Vitamin Water I drank earlier.

"Hey, it's okay. I understand. Let me go explain to the guys and we'll figure out a plan. I'll get you home before your mom arrives. But maybe, I don't know, maybe we should tell her about Evan and Livi? And about us?"

"Yeah. I'll tell her," I promise, giving Asher a shaky grin. "I just need to find the right moment. And the right words. She's probably not going to be overly impressed. You know, timing-wise. And she's going to want to know how we met. I don't know if 'he stopped me on the side of the road' is really something that's going to make her feel comfortable."

"We'll worry about that later. For now, let's figure out how we're going to get out of here and get you home."

"Thanks, Ash."

"I've got you, Shaeline."

Even though I want to believe him, that sick feeling in my stomach still stays. I brush it off as hunger, tiredness, and the overwhelming nature of everything I've been experiencing and vow to go find somewhere with a little bit of food before we head back to Emerald Beach. If a greasy, waterfront hot dog can't fix me, I don't think anything can.

Chapter Fourteen

ASHER

I can't believe how fast things can fall apart.

Shae tells me she's running off to get something to eat during part of our next set, and I don't see her back until after we've finished the final song. Before we went on, I quickly explained to the guys the situation and agreed to leave my guitar for Chance to play so he and Gabe can do a set alone to end the night. We'll have enough time in between the final two for Gabe to drop Shae and me off at the condo to get my car, and hopefully everything will be okay. It doesn't help the panicky feeling in my chest, however, knowing that Shae might get into trouble because of my idea for her to come to Tampa with us. Maybe I should have made sure she asked her mom.

Maybe we should have been more responsible. Thought things through. Not got caught up in the summer and the sea.

When I get off the soundstage after the second set, Shae's standing next to the speakers with a little frown on her face. I don't understand why she looks so upset until two people approach us before I have a chance to say anything. It's the guy and girl from Barracuda's, the two I saw the first day I was in Emerald Beach after running into Shae on the side of the road. I thought that they were supposed to be in Europe or something, going on their own version of a tour for the summer. But here they are, standing in front of us in Tampa, and Shae looks like she might start to cry.

"That was a great set! I loved the last song. What's that one called again?"

I open my mouth to answer and maybe to ask the question as to what exactly they're doing here and why they're trying to have a discussion with us, but Shae cuts into the awkward attempt at conversation. "I thought you guys were backpacking in Europe?"

Livi tosses her curls behind her shoulder, casting a quick gaze over at Evan who is trying hard to look like it wasn't his idea to come over here in the first place. "Oh, that fell through. We decided to come spend some time here instead. Funny seeing you here. With—I'm sorry, how do you know each other?"

I want to tell Livi and Evan that Shae and I are more in love than the two of them ever could be, but I keep my mouth shut because this isn't my place to get involved. At least, not yet.

"What?" Shae sounds incredulous. "This is Asher and we—you know what? It doesn't matter. I have nothing to say to either one of you, and neither of you have any right to know anything about my life anymore."

"Wait," Evan says, and I can see the gears turning in his head as he thinks for a moment about what to say next. He almost looks offended when he asks his question. "Are you two like, yeah?"

Shae flicks her gaze to me only for a second, and I spot the fury in her eyes immediately. I place a hand on her back gently, and break into the talk. "I think maybe it would be best if we didn't get into this conversation. It was nice to meet you both, but I think we need to—"

"Hang on." Shae wrinkles her eyebrows together. "What if we are? What's it to you, Evan?"

Livi suddenly seems to decide that escaping from the discussion is the best course of action, sliding her hand into Evan's. He almost doesn't let her because his fists are clenched so hard against his sides. "Evan? We should go, maybe. There's going to be more shows starting soon and I want to get a good seat."

Evan ignores Livi entirely, even though he's holding her hand and she's practically dragging him away from the soundstage. "Do you even know this guy, Shae? Like, where's he even from? You're seeing a traveling musician? He probably gets a girl in every city and—"

"Evan! Let's go!" Livi has the right idea, but the wrong approach. My approach right now is about akin to punching Evan in the face, but I don't want to get cited for assault even though, in my opinion, the guy deserves it.

"And what?" Shae asks, clearly trying to keep her shaking voice as calm as possible so she doesn't stir up a scene.

"I'm sure you know what these guys are like, Shae. They're nothing, they're not any better than a one-night stand."

My fingers twitch, but I keep them planted against the fabric of Shae's shirt. The sensation of her body against my hand is the only thing keeping me from totally losing it.

"That must make you an awfully shit person, Evan. I mean, you cheated on me with my best friend. At least Asher isn't—"

"Isn't what?" Evan hisses, daring her to say more. Livi tugs hard on his hand just then and seemingly breaks his angry spell. He glares at her for distracting him, his gaze the only thing that was holding him to our conversation. "Never mind, Shae. You're not worth it. This whole discussion isn't worth it."

"You're the ones who came over here." The words fall from Shae's mouth and I start to feel my heart pound, the level of resentment I have for Livi and Evan rising with every passing second.

"And I regret it."

"Good. Then why don't you leave?"

Evan looks over at Livi, who is all red in the face. "Let's get out of here. What a waste of breath."

The two of them give Shae and me a glance over before Livi pulls Evan out into the crowd of people milling about by the soundstage, and within moments they disappear into the throngs of people and darkness.

I can feel Shae vibrating with anger through the spot where my hand is touching her.

"You okay?" I ask, trying to turn her attention back toward me instead of off into the crowd. "Shae?"

"Yeah." She breathes out, hard. "I just...I guess I didn't expect to see them again before I went to school. I thought maybe I could avoid the two of them for the rest of my life. Turns out Florida is smaller than I ever thought."

Trailing my fingers along her back to meet the spot where Shae's elbow touches her side, I give her a gentle nudge. "Let's go for a walk. Stretch our legs. We'll just make sure we're headed in the opposite direction of them."

Shae nods, even though before we go, she looks back toward where Evan and Livi have walked off to.

The rest of the night passes with no further incidents, though the atmosphere around Shae is stormy. She's clearly been affected by seeing Evan and Livi again and catching them in their lie or misunderstanding or whatever it is that caused them to not actually be in Europe away from her life with me. Gabe chatters all the way to his car, and I fill in the quiet with responses to his questions and hype around playing in front of a crowd for the first time in just over a week. Shae remains quiet, probably stewing over the altercation, which I can understand. I'm upset for her.

Gabe speeds through the streets of Tampa toward Genesis Lake and drops us off at the condo with a little time to spare. We rush up to my place to gather Shae's things before I take her down into the parking garage to my car, where we load up and take off into the night. She doesn't talk much all the way back to Emerald Beach; instead, we listen to old music on the radio, and I hum along with the melodies I know. She stares out of the window at the night for most of the drive, only breaking her gaze out at the trees and the stars when I place my hand on top of hers. Then she gives me a half-smile, and a sigh.

"I'm sorry to make you miss the last set."

I tap my fingers on the steering wheel. "Don't worry about it. Seriously. Getting you home for your mom's arrival is much more important to me right now."

The headlights blaze out across the empty road, the darkness and the moonlight all mixed together and surrounding us. We turn onto Mermaid Avenue with a half hour to spare before Shae's mom is supposed to be home, but there's something that's not quite right when I turn into the driveway. The glow of the streetlamps combined with the reflection off the windows shows me a shadow standing on the porch of the house, and immediately my stomach tumbles into my shoes.

"Is that—" I begin to ask, but I realize I already know the answer. Shae's face loses color in the night, and as I shift the car reluctantly into park, the figure approaches and taps at the driver's side window. Pressing the button on the door, I roll it down halfway, to see Shae's mother standing out in the night.

"Shaeline, where have you been? Who is this?"

Shae sinks so far into the bucket seat of the car I think she's trying to disappear, while her mom looks me over with some kind of dismay. Her eyes find my tattoos in the night, and I know with my ripped jeans and ink I'm not exactly the look she was hoping for her daughter.

"Mom, Asher. Asher, my mom. We were out for a drive and—"

Her mother holds up one hand before gesturing for us to get out of the car. "Out, both of you, now. In the house."

I twist off the ignition and step out into the warm Florida air, while Shae slinks around the side of the vehicle. Letting her lead the way into the house, I follow behind as she unlocks the door and lets us into the cool darkness. Shae's mother flips on a light, leaves her suitcases by the front door, and doesn't even take her shoes off before she begins to ask her questions.

"Where were you, Shaeline? I've been home for over an hour."

"You said you were going to be here at midnight." Shae grapples for something to hold on to in the conversation, but it's clear even to me that we're totally caught.

"And you said you were home. You didn't answer my question. Where have you been?"

"I was just out with Asher and we went for a drive and—"

Mrs. Samson flicks her gaze to me. "Right, and who are you?"

"Asher Lohan, ma'am—"

"Shaeline, you were out in the middle of the night with a boy I don't even know? What would Evan think of that? Did Livi put you up to this? I always told you that the quiet ones are the most trouble."

Shae stiffens at the two names, and I can practically feel her heart pounding in anger from the entryway. It only takes a moment before she deflates, and all the details about what happened the weeks before come spilling out.

"Evan and I—well, Evan broke up with me. The day you left. He'd been cheating on me with Livi. And then on the way home I ran into Asher and his bandmates and we talked for a minute and then the next morning when I got fired from Beaches N' Cream for something stupid that Evan did, they were there, too, and we hung out and it just...I don't know, Mom. Asher and I kind of hit it off. We've been spending some time together."

Her mother wrinkles her forehead, and it's clear to me she doesn't know what to feel about everything her daughter's just said. "Some time together" is kind of an understatement, but I suppose that Mrs. Samson doesn't need to know the tiny details of how I've been sleeping in her daughter's bed and she's recently started sleeping in mine.

"So, wait. Let me make sure I understand this correctly. Evan broke up with you for Livi and you didn't think to telephone me at Will's to let me know about this? Even if it wasn't anything to do with Livi, I'd still want to know. I could have come home. We could have had a conversation about things. You didn't have to go run off with a stranger and try and—I don't even know, Shaeline."

"I didn't run off with a stranger, Mom. Asher's different."

Shae's mother looks over at me, glued to my spot on the space between the tiled floor and the hardwood one. Her gaze is piercing, like she's a wolf and she's getting ready to attack me as her prey for hurting one of her babies. "How are you different from the other twenty-year-olds in this town, Asher?"

It's a loaded question that I know I'm not supposed to answer, but for some stupid reason, I try.

"I—I'm in love with her."

All the air gets sucked out of the room, the stillness of the night becoming even more quiet, as if that were possible. Nobody says anything for at least ten seconds, allowing the atmosphere to absorb what it is I've just thrown out into it. Shae stares at me with her mouth practically hanging open, as if she can't believe I've just told her mother that within the first few minutes of meeting her.

To be fair, I can't believe I did it either. But I've never felt for someone the way I feel about Shae, and something in my heart wants the whole world to know.

Mrs. Samson rubs her head as if she's tired of the conversation and it's giving her a migraine. I used to see the same from my own mother when I'd do something that would annoy her so badly she'd have to take a pain reliever. "You're in love with her?"

"Yes, ma'am."

"You can cut out the 'ma'am' from this conversation, Asher. Since Shaeline doesn't want to tell me, I'm expecting you to give me the rundown as to where you were tonight."

I look over at Shae who rocks from foot to foot, antsy for either the truth to come out, or her potential punishment to be revealed for doing something she wasn't supposed to do with a person she probably wasn't supposed to know in the first place.

"We were in Tampa. I'm on tour with my band and—"

"Tampa?"

"Yes, ma—yes. We're performing in the Buskers Festival. I asked Shae to come with me. She actually performed on stage tonight during our warmup. The crowd really enjoyed her improvisation."

Mrs. Samson frowns, deep lines creasing in her forehead. "You're on tour with a band?"

I'm digging myself a hole in the sand, but I can't stop responding now because said hole will just fill with water. "I am, yes. I play guitar with two cousins from Genesis Lake."

"You took my daughter, without my permission, to Tampa, after her boyfriend just broke up with her for her best friend? Do you not think about how awful that sounds, you taking advantage of a girl who is emotional over the—"

"Mom!" Shae finally cuts in, finding her voice amongst the noise. "It wasn't Asher's fault. We decided to go together. I wanted to go. It had nothing to do with Evan and Livi and everything to do with the fact that I'm in love with him too."

My heart soars at hearing her admit to her mother that she has more than just a fleeting interest in me. Even though I knew she loved me, and even though I knew I loved her, too, having her say it to her mom feels different—like we've just opened the door to some other stage in the relationship.

But it's clear from her reaction that Shae's mother doesn't see it the same way.

"In love? You've known each other for all of two minutes, Shaeline—"

"And maybe that's all it takes!" Shae's voice gets more and more insistent, creeping up in volume. "When you and Dad were together you used to tell me the stories about how you both met, and it didn't take much longer than that for you two to get married."

"And look how that turned out. We've been divorced for four years. Just because you think you're in love in the moment doesn't mean you're really in it for the long haul."

"Mom, this is different. This is—"

Shae's mother looks over at me again, and the feeling of being nervous comes back. I thought maybe I'd be able to disappear into the backdrop of the wall and sneak out the front door maybe when the time was right and Shae seemed to have things under control, but it doesn't look like that's going to be possible anymore. Plus, leaving wouldn't be very supportive—even though I'm worried about what's going to come next.

"What about for you? Is this different than those groupies you get at your shows?"

The idea of Collide having groupies at our little festivals around Florida is amusing, and I fight off the tiny grin that's rumbling around in my head because this is much more serious.

"I can't even put it into words, Mrs. Samson."

Shae smiles at me and my response, but her mother's expression doesn't soften. "You'd better find some words really quick because I'm running a countdown in my head and so far, I'd say you've got about five seconds left to change my mind."

"I—I've never had a real girlfriend before," I admit, readying everything I should have said to Shae before but didn't find the opportunity to. "I met Shae and it's like the whole world just fell into place. I know the timing wasn't the best, but don't they say that good things happen when you least expect them? I couldn't have asked for someone better. A better summer. Someone even more—"

Mrs. Samson holds up one hand again, and I pause to take a breath. "That's enough, Asher. I think it's about time for you to go."

"But—" Shae speaks up, taking a step toward me like she's going to hold on so I can't leave.

"Shaeline, we need to have a conversation, and it's a conversation we're going to have now. Alone."

I give Shae a weak little smile and mouth that everything's going to be okay. In my head I also kiss her, but now isn't the time for displays of affection like that. Instead, I nod and back out of the front door into the night air, leaving Shae and her mom in the house. I'm just about to leave when I remember that I have Shae's suitcase in the back of the car, so I lift it out and carry it to the front alcove of the entryway and tuck it behind a post so it's not visible from the road. Before I pull out of the drive, I drop her a text to let her know what I've done, and then I shift the car into reverse and make my way down Mermaid Avenue.

The drive back to Tampa is lonely, and I don't even bother listening to anything on the radio because I feel like I need the silence after a night like this.

Chapter Fifteen

SHAE

It's painful to watch the front door close, Asher stepping out into the night and disappearing in the dark. I know he's immediately going to be back on his way to Tampa to finish off the shows he and Gabe and Chance have planned for the rest of the Buskers Festival, meaning I'll be stuck here in Emerald Beach alone for the foreseeable future. The idea of being away from Asher makes me feel sick to my stomach; we've been nearly inseparable since the afternoon we spent on the beach and at Barracuda's. The idea of being alone in my bed without his quiet breathing to lull me to sleep is uncomfortable at best.

"Shaeline, you've got some explaining to do." My mother's voice cuts into my staring at the entryway, hoping Asher will come back in and whisk me away. "Go sit in the living room. I'll be in shortly."

I don't stick around to ask any questions. Instead, I escape as fast as possible into the dark room and flick on the lamp next to the piano for a dim glow in the midnight atmosphere. I curl myself up on the couch with a pillow in my lap, feeling like maybe I can hide behind it if I just try hard enough. The phone in my back pocket feels like a brick, and I pull it out and set it down on the table where it flashes once with a message that says "Asher" on the screen. I don't dare pick it up.

It takes Mom forever to show up in the doorway of the living room, but when she does, she's holding two cups of lemonade. Setting one down on the table for me, she holds on to the other and seats herself in the armchair across the room from the piano bench.

"So, when were you going to tell me that you met a new boy and were feeling serious about him? And, on top of that, when were you going to tell me about Evan?"

Biting the inside of my cheek, I heave in a deep breath. "I don't know. I got all caught up in everything. Evan and Livi were both at Barracuda's when I went to meet Evan after you got the taxi, and that's when they told me about what was going on. I ran into Asher on the way home, then again outside of Beaches N' Cream—"

"Speaking of your job, what happened there? You were let go on your first day? Surely, it's something Laura and I can work out. I'm sure whatever it was could have been handled differently."

There's no easy way to tell your mother that your ex-boyfriend made up a story about you losing your virginity to him inside of his parents' ice cream parlor, so for a moment, I don't say anything. I hope the question just dissolves into nothingness, but it doesn't because Mom's still sitting there across the room from me waiting for me to fill her in on what exactly caused me to lose my job that was supposed to pay for my college textbooks.

"Evan, um...he kind of made up a rumor about us."

"What kind of rumor? You can't possibly be telling me that some piece of gossip caused you to lose your position at Beaches N' Cream? Laura and Evan's father surely have more sense than that. What was it about?"

I stare at Mom for a couple of seconds, thinking about what Evan told his mother and hoping I'm able to transfer it to her telepathically so I don't have to use the words out loud. Of course, it doesn't work.

"Shae?" She wrinkles her brow.

"It was...the rumor was about us. Being together. Like, *together*. In Beaches N' Cream while it was closed."

My mother nearly chokes on her lemonade. "You mean he said you had intercourse in the ice cream parlor?"

I nod, cringing. The memory suddenly feels fresh again, and salty tears prickle at the corners of my eyes.

"That's not a reason for them to fire you, especially if it's not true." There's silence for a second, like she's waiting for me to confirm that it isn't. But if I say I didn't sleep with Evan, which I didn't, it doesn't mean I didn't sleep with Asher, which I did. Thankfully, after a few moments of awkwardness, she continues her thought. "It doesn't matter whether you did or you didn't or whatnot. They had no right to do that, I don't think."

"It's fine, Mom. I'm over it."

"You don't look like you're over it, Shae."

"It just—I am. I'm over it and I'm over Evan. I'm not over the fact that he hurt me, but that's something entirely different."

Then, to my surprise, my mother gives me a little half-smile before taking another sip of her lemonade. "I know what you're saying. I feel like I'm over Will already, but the fact that I got up to Canada and—well, it doesn't matter now. My feelings are hurt but I don't want to think about him anymore. He's not worth my energy."

"Basically." I finally unfreeze from my position behind the couch cushion and reach for my lemonade to drink a mouthful. We sit in the quiet of the room for a little while, the sour taste of the yellowy juice sticking in my mouth in the heat. I don't look at Mom except for the occasional little peek, instead mentally ghost-playing the piano with one of the songs that Asher and I wrote over the week we spent here alone.

"I'm sorry I wasn't here to help you go through all that."

I shrug, setting my lemonade glass down on the table again. "It's okay. You had your own stuff going on. I handled it. And Asher helped."

Mom gives me a little, twisted look like she's about to say something negative, but I cut her off.

"He really did, Mom. Not just as a distraction either. You know when you think your whole life is falling apart and then you just, I don't know, it just turns all around in a second like all those bad things were happening for a reason? That's what it feels like happened to me. Evan cheated on me, Livi turned out to be a bad friend, but then I met Asher and he plays music and we're really, truly...we like each other a lot."

Mom leans back in her chair with a deep breath. "Sounds like you've had a special few days. But I did tell you not to leave town. And I would have expected you to be mature enough to contact me when these things happened."

"I know." I start biting the inside of my lip again, because I know there's a punishment coming that I'm probably not going to like.

"But I also know that in two months you're going to be in Tampa on your own for school. And I can't hold on to you with rules forever."

The statement takes me by surprise. "What do you mean?"

"I mean that I'm upset with your choices, and while you're under the roof of this house you're going to need to abide by the rules I set up. When I tell you that you're not to do something, you don't do it."

"Okay."

"As you know, normally your punishment would be not seeing Evan or Livi or leaving the house, but I have a feeling that you don't want to see them anyway. And I presume Asher's on his way back to Tampa so you won't be seeing him either. So, I'm at a bit of a loss here of what to do with you, Shaeline. Other than chores. We have a list an arm's length long that we can tackle together."

"We actually ran into Evan and Livi in Tampa," I admit, the memory of earlier in the evening suddenly coming to mind as I stifle a yawn. "And you're right, I don't want to see them anyway. Not anymore."

Mom hums, untucking a leg from underneath herself and adjusting her position in the oversized chair. "We can decide later what you're going to do to make up for things. Weeding the garden might be a good start. Head on off to bed, I'm going to get some laundry on."

I scamper off out of the living room without another word, picking up my phone on the way, and head down the hallway to my room where I immediately close the door and flop down on the bed sheets. The fabric smells like Asher, and I roll my body over the coverlet until I'm lying down on top of the mattress entirely. It takes me a second to remember that I have a message on my phone, and I hold the device precariously above my face and poke at the screen.

> ASHER: *I left your suitcase on the front porch. Was in the back of the car. Hope you don't get in too much trouble. Text me later, if you want.*

It feels empty here in this room without Asher next to me. Thinking of what exactly to say, I flip over and prop up my phone on the pillows before I tap back a note in my messages application.

> SHAE: *I'm sorry you got dragged into that. I honestly didn't know it was going to turn out the way it did. I figured I could break things to Mom a different way rather than all at once in a big surprise like that.*

> SHAE: *Also, my pillows smell like your shampoo still.*

I suspect Asher's still driving and that I won't get a response until he's back in Genesis Lake, but a moment later, three little dots appear on the screen that tell me he's typing something.

> ASHER: *It's okay. I just hope I didn't make things worse. I'll be back at the condo in twenty minutes—I'll call you then.*

I'm tired, but not tired enough to not want to talk to Asher. After changing into a pair of soft shorts and a heavier tank top, I curl up underneath the blankets, forcing myself to stay awake by playing tic-tac-toe on my phone over and over again. It's thirty-two minutes later that his name pops up on the device, pulsating silently to let me know he's calling.

"Hi," I whisper, trying to keep my voice low so Mom won't know I'm still awake.

"Hey." There's some rustling around in the background and I immediately identify it as Asher getting into bed himself. "Sorry I'm late, Gabe texted and wanted to know if everything was okay and to let me know about the last set."

"It's okay."

There's silence then, for a few moments, like neither of us has any idea of what to say. It feels like we both need or want to talk about what happened only a couple of hours ago with Mom, but neither of us knows where to start the conversation. Thankfully, Asher thinks up something before the call falls into total awkwardness.

"Was everything okay with your mom after I left? How much trouble are you in?"

"Surprisingly little, in comparison to what I thought I'd be in. I have to weed the garden and probably do chores until I leave for college, but it could have been a whole lot worse. I think she figures I've already been punished by this whole summer."

Asher's chuckle trickles through the phone. "Hey, it's not all bad."

"I thought it was about to turn that way when we pulled up the driveway and Mom came to the car window. She looked more upset than I've seen her in a long time."

"She was probably just worried for you, Shae. That's what parents do. They worry about their kids driving up in the middle of the night with some stranger they've never heard of before."

I try to hold in another yawn, but it doesn't work as well as it did the first time when I was out in the living room with Mom.

"Tired?" Asher asks. "I'm in bed too. It feels like today's gone on forever."

"I know. But I want to talk to you. We aren't going to see each other until after the Buskers Festival, are we?"

"Probably not. With rehearsing and all that during the day, and then playing at night, I'm not sure I could swing a four-hour round trip and still be able to perform at night."

"It's okay," I reply, but it feels like it isn't. I haven't been without Asher for more than a few hours since we met, and over a week is almost the same as being told we won't see each other for a century. "We can still text. And wait, you'll come back after the Festival, right?"

A pause comes from Asher's end of the line, and this tells me something.

"What's wrong, Ash?"

"Well." The word is long and dragged out and sounds like its own separate sentence from whatever else Asher's going to say. "When I was talking to Gabe, he said that a guy from Black Horse Records pulled him aside after the set and asked about the band."

"What's Black Horse Records?"

"A small, independent label out of Tampa. Gabe had sent them some information and a recording a while back and never heard anything. Guess we just assumed they forgot about us. They probably get thousands of samples. But I guess it's just kind of a fluke that the manager of the label was there tonight, and he heard us play. Stuck around for a set and then came back to Gabe later to strike up a conversation about a contract. This—this never happens."

"But that's amazing!" I try to sound upbeat because I'm so thrilled for Collide and their music is fantastic; however, some selfish part of me wants Asher to come back to Emerald Beach and spend the remainder of the summer with me.

"So, that's my dilemma. I need to stay here to deal with the contract stuff with the guys and finish our festival gigs. After the Buskers Festival is August Mania over in St. Pete's, and then after that I'm supposed to be in Miami…" Asher trails off, and I don't reply because it sounds like he doesn't want me to. He has a busy summer without me, and now with a recording label interested in their music, it sounds like Collide's really going to start taking off.

"What does this mean?" I ask quietly, salty tears prickling at the corners of my eyes and telling me what I already know. Asher's gone.

"It means—can you convince your mom to let you come back to Tampa? You can come on tour with us for the summer and we can work things out for September? You can move into your dorm early, get comfortable with campus—it's a thing, probably?"

A droplet falls down my cheek as I shake my head even though Asher can't see. "It's definitely not going to happen."

We don't say anything for a bit, just listening to the sounds of each other breathing on the line. Every bit of me that was tired is wide awake now, and silent tears slip down my face as quickly as I can brush them away. After all this time, I thought the summer was coming around, but it's only getting back to ruining me again.

"Shae?" Asher says, his voice like an echo in the darkness. "Are you still awake?"

"Yeah."

"I love you."

All the air gets sucked out of the room and I choke out a sob before replying.

"I know."

Chapter Sixteen

ASHER

Where the first day in Tampa flew by, the remainder of them pass slowly. The time I'm not performing with Gabe and Chance, I'm locked up in my condo with my guitar, writing more songs inspired by distance, or just tweaking the notes for "Mermaid Avenue." Music is the only thing that distracts me from the fact Shae's not with me and Gabe spends every spare moment reviewing the contract for the band with Black Horse Records, trying to find a flaw. Even though I text and talk on the phone with Shae every evening, there are nights when I don't get home until late because of a set or a conversation or a gathering of other Buskers musicians. The time gets later and later until one day when it's two in the morning and I'm still up toying with lyrics.

The next morning, I sleep through rehearsal at Gabe and Chance's along with another review of the contract language. I expect sixty missed calls and texts, but all I wake up to is a message from Gabe saying to take all the time I need. Somehow, he understands better than I anticipated he would. Chance, however, is another story. He teases me when we're together, but he's turned to silence when we're apart. It's becoming a little strange, like maybe we aren't connecting in the way we used to.

It's a scorching Friday night when we're packing up from our final set of the evening, stowing away our instruments and collecting our discarded water bottles, when a redhead from the next soundstage over waves us down. Her name's something different—Storm, I think—but I honestly haven't paid much attention to the girls surrounding Gabe and Chance after we're done performing. Storm, though, she doesn't seem to be much interested in spending the night with either of them. This only makes them both want her more.

"Asher!" she calls, and I can't help but wonder how she even knows my name. "We're throwing a little party at our hotel suite. Y'all should come."

Storm's one of those girls who tours for the hell of it, her parents paying off her expenses so she'll stay out of their hair for the summer. She hasn't told me that or anything, I've figured it out on my own, mainly because she just threw around the term "hotel suite" instead of "hostel" or "shared, four-person room" like it was free Halloween candy.

I zip my guitar case shut and stand it right-side up as I rise from my crouching position. "I don't know, a party's not really my scene. You should ask Gabe or Chance though."

My gaze flickers over to the other two band members who are engaged in conversation with a group of girls who appear to all be around our ages. When I glance back at Storm, she's chuckling.

"As if those two would even notice me popping into their conversation right now. Come on, you know you want to come. Something to get your mind off whatever it is you're thinking of."

The thing is, I don't want to get my mind off Shae. In fact, I want my mind to stay firmly planted on her until I'm able to get back to Emerald Beach. Which, knowing the tour schedule for the rest of the month, might not be for a while.

"Plus, I'll supply the beer. You don't even have to spot me or pay me back. We can say it's a celebration for the contract with Black Horse." Storm smiles, tossing a red wave over her shoulder. The way she's styled her hair reminds me a little of Shae on the first day we met, and it makes my nostalgia feel a little stronger. I haven't had a beer since an earlier leg of the tour, but what I'd really like right about now is a Frozen Rocket from Barracuda's.

However, I can't spend another night sulking in my condo. Gabe and Chance will drag me out kicking and screaming to wherever it is they're going, and I'd much rather end up at Storm's hotel suite with some other musicians than act as a third wheel to some groupie adventure. Plus, they've already told her about the contract at some point, so I guess I have to go along to my own celebration. It would be rude if I didn't.

"Sure, why not?" I rub my hand over my jaw, hoping the words come out less reluctant than how I feel. "I'll let them know whenever—when they're done with whatever it is they're doing."

Storm smiles, her dark eyes glistening under the light of the overhead lamps. "Awesome! We're headed there now—The Park Royal. I'm in 1501, fifteenth floor. And if they can't come, you should come anyway. I have a feeling you could use a night out."

She takes off before I can say anything more, turning on the heel of her shoe and disappearing into the dark.

"Was that Storm? What's she doing tonight?" Chance appears over my shoulder, Gabe still engaged with the collection of girls over by the corner of the stage.

"Invited us to a party at her suite. She's headed back there now so we can show up whenever, I guess."

"Hell yes. You know what they say about redheads and—"

"I don't, and I don't think anyone says what you're about to say except you, Chance."

He punches me in the arm, and I nearly drop my guitar on the boardwalk just as Gabe finds his way over to where we're standing, and I have to tell him what Storm came over and said as well. He doesn't seem as overly thrilled as Chance at the idea of the party, but he's always been a bit more subdued when he's interested in someone. Maybe he thinks that if he doesn't act super interested then we won't notice that he's trying to catch someone's attention. It never works, but I've never bothered to call him out on it.

"Well, let's pack this stuff up and drive it home before we get to the hotel. I'd kind of like to shower, honestly, after being under all those lights." Gabe tightens his bun, snapping the elastic on his hair to make a little pouf at the back of his head. "And Chance, you could use one. Bad."

Chance rolls his eyes at his cousin, picking up one of his small, handheld drums and placing it in his backpack for safekeeping. We collect our instruments a few moments later, along with all the cords and supplies we've brought on our own, leaving the soundstage for tomorrow when we play our set again for a new, and busier, crowd.

The entire drive back to Genesis Lake and my condo, I think about the words in my new song, "Imagination." It's something I've been working on in my spare time, and I feel like I've almost started having a breakthrough with the words when Gabe pulls the van up to my place and shoves the vehicle into park. He never parks, he just idles. And that's when I know that something's wrong.

"Gabe?" I say his name slowly, and he turns the radio down before he responds with a sigh. Chance stares straight ahead, out of the front windshield, into the bright headlights casting a glow on the side of the condo building.

"Listen, Asher. I didn't want to have to tell you this, but I don't really think there's going to be a good time. I kept waiting for one, but it still hasn't come yet, and we've really got to sign this contract."

"So, we'll sign it. If you think it's solid, I trust you. I'll put my name to it."

An emptiness fills the interior of the van, telling me the part about my name is the part that's going to be an issue.

"See, here's the thing." Gabe's jaw twitches in the dim light of the inside of the vehicle. He really doesn't want to tell me whatever it is that he's about to say.

"What thing?"

"Ash—the guy from Black Horse came by while you were driving Shae home. He only saw me and Chance play. When I told him there was a third guy—you—he didn't really agree to having a third person in the band.

He just wants to sign the two of us since Chance can play guitar too."

My heart stops beating for a moment, hiccupping against my ribcage. The band that I've been part of for so long finally gets offered an opportunity of a lifetime, and I'm just out of reach. I'm not there. I'm driving Shae home to Emerald Beach, the only place I've ever wanted to be with the only person I ever wanted to be with. But the second thing I've wanted, always, is to play music. And I can't help the gnawing feeling in my chest that I've just ruined something. Everything. By not being here. By leaving Shae home. I need both.

"You're saying that—you mean... The contract doesn't even have my name on it, does it?"

The absolute lack of response tells me everything I need to know. I slide open the door of the van and collect my guitar from the side of the seat. Rage boils up in my stomach, sitting like fire in my throat. If I say anything, I'm going to regret it, or I'm going to explode. So, I don't. Not entirely.

"Have *fun* celebrating at Storm's." I shut the door to the rickety old van and walk inside without another word, all the while thinking about the fact that my friends have just sold out.

When I get up to my condo, I leave my guitar by the front door and lock the latch before heading straight for my bedroom. I don't want to be awake any more today, I don't want to go to Storm's party and watch Gabe and Chance hit on her and whoever else is there. I want to be with Shae. I want to talk to her. I want to feel the way she touches my skin and the electricity that comes from the feelings we have inside for each other. I contemplate driving back to Emerald Beach tonight, but when I pull out my phone it's already past midnight. Instead, I fire off a text to Shae before I hop in the shower to wash off the spotlight I probably don't even deserve.

ASHER: *Can we talk?*

Ten minutes later, I'm dripping on the bedroom rug, a towel tied around my waist as I check my messages.

SHAE: *Call me whenever. I'll be awake. I miss you.*

ASHER: *Now?*

SHAE: *Okay.*

I hit the green button in the corner of the screen next to her name, and the phone barely rings once before she picks up the line.

"Hey," she whispers, and I know she's trying to be quiet so her mom doesn't overhear that she's on the phone so late. "What's going on?"

There's a heat rising from my chest to behind my eyes as I take a seat on my unmade bed, scooting myself to the middle of the mattress. Before I respond, I allow myself to collapse on my pillows that still somehow smell like Shae's jasmine shampoo.

"Asher? Did something happen?"

"The contract…" I stumble over the words, not really sure how to put them into a proper sentence. It feels like if I do, then everything about the situation will be true, when I really want it to be a lie. "The contract from Black

Horse Records. They don't want me. They only want Gabe and Chance."

I can practically picture Shae wrinkling her eyebrows together. "What do you mean, they don't want you?"

"The manager saw the band play when I went to drive you home that night. He doesn't think they need two people in the group who can play guitar. Chance already proved to him that he's good enough to keep up with Gabe. They didn't even put my name on the contract. It was just Gabe and Chance all along, and it took the guys until now to let me know."

"Oh. Oh, no. I'm so sorry, Ash. I don't even know what to say to make things better."

I take in a deep breath and then sigh it all out at once. "I don't know either. I guess I just wanted to talk to you. Knowing you're listening makes me feel better."

"How angry are you right now?"

"I'm not sure how to measure it. I just...I can't even put it into words. Usually when something like this happens, I'd write a song about it or play guitar or something. But I don't have anything to say. I just feel like all my dreams have been smashed into a thousand pieces. How can I even go on stage with them tomorrow night? And tomorrow's going to be our busiest night. What will I say? I mean, the atmosphere's going to be all wrong."

"You can't not go." There's some rustling on the other end of the line as Shae presumably adjusts herself in her bed, her voice still hushed. "You have to be bigger than them. You have to stand up there on that stage knowing you deserve to be there too. Just because they might be signing on with a label in the future doesn't mean that the people in the crowd who came to hear you play know it's closing in on your last show together. It doesn't mean you can't play on your own, be a solo artist, find another band. You have so much talent, Ash."

"Not enough for Black Horse."

"They didn't even see you play. You can't say that."

She's right, I can't, but it's the way I feel. I breathe in a deep sigh of cool condo air and roll over on the bed to face the large windows overlooking the water in the distance.

"I miss you. I wish you were here," I say. The dampness of my hair leaves a wet spot on one of my pillows, and I trade it off for the one that smells like Shae's shampoo. It's probably not truly the case, a figment of my imagination since I've washed these sheets since she left. But in my head the scent of her is here with me and it helps.

"I miss you too. When do you think we'll be able to see each other again? What about St. Pete's? What about everything? I mean, you guys had shows..."

"I don't know. I honestly don't. I guess that must be in the contract somewhere. Maybe we'll be allowed to finish off the summer with what we had planned. At this point, though, I don't know if I want to. I kind of want to be done with it all. Let them tour on their own for the summer while I find a job in Tampa."

Shae doesn't respond for a few moments, but she's breathing on the other end of the line loud enough for me to hear the steady rhythm.

"This isn't the summer either of us had planned, I don't think. I mean, with Evan and Livi and your contract and me practically being grounded like a twelve-year-old.

I expected long days on the beach in the sand and nights at Barracuda's. Instead, we're getting nights with whispered telephone calls and friends who aren't who they say they are. There are good things, though, even if they're hard to see right now."

"Like what?" I scoff, my tone a bit harsher than I really want it to be, even though I'm wallowing in a state of self-pity and frustration.

"Like us," Shae replies. "This is an unexpected summer. The summer of surprises and feelings and firsts. The summer of the moments in between. The summer I loved you."

As soon as she says those words, lyrics start to flow into my mind.

"Hang on, I need to grab my guitar."

"What? Asher, it's one in the morning. Get some sleep."

"No, wait. I have an idea. Just—just bear with me."

I set the phone down on the bed before I retie my towel around my waist. I half run to the front door to grab my guitar from the spot where I left it. When I get back to the bedroom, I poke the speakerphone button so I can play and have Shae hear at the same time.

"Shae?" I check the sound.

"I'm here."

"I think I've just thought up a song. Let me know what you think."

Strumming a couple of chords, my fingers dance across the strings of the guitar as I sing.

Surprise

I fell in love

For the first time

Maybe the last time

And surprise

It's not the way

I expected or

She expected but

Surprise

We tripped over all the

Moments that are in between

And I said hello

Hello to the summer I loved you

And goodbye

To the places I thought I'd never go

And surprise

To the feelings I never knew I'd ever keep

All because I said hello

Hello to the summer I loved you

Chapter Seventeen

SHAE

I think this is the first Saturday I've ever hated. I sleep in until well after ten and wake up with a splitting headache. Mom tries to make light conversation at breakfast, but it's clear she's still mad about me jaunting around with Asher, and neither she nor I make any effort to keep the talk going once it dies away. We wash the breakfast dishes in near total silence until she names my first punishment of the day: weeding out the flower beds along the sidewalk. I barely remembered they existed until she mentions them.

The sun is already hot in the sky when I finally drag myself out of the door with some gardening gloves tucked opposite my phone in my back pocket. I also bring Mom's garden pad for kneeling on and a random hat that was sitting on my desk. Only when I go to put it on do I realize it's the one Asher loaned me one night while we were sitting on the back patio, and I feel sick to my stomach. This is the longest we've been apart since we met for the second time; how is it that being away from someone I only met a couple of weeks ago can make me feel this terrible?

I drop the foam pad on the white sidewalk and kneel to stick my head between a couple of flowering bushes I couldn't name if you paid me. The answer is that I'm worried about Asher, about what he's going to do about the contract, and where he's going to go when the band breaks up. He talked about finding a job in Tampa, presumably since it's so close to Genesis Lake, but what if he decides to go somewhere else to get away from everything? I rip a large weed free of the ground and absently shake loose dirt from the roots before tossing it into the growing pile behind me.

Wild ideas chase their way around my brain while I twist and tug at the stubborn weeds. We haven't been very active in the yard this year and it shows; the green stalks are thick, tough, and determined to stay put. Their pungent smells mix with thoughts of what sorts of jobs Asher might be able to get in Tampa, or maybe even here in Emerald Beach or a little farther in Emerald City. My stomach does another flip at that thought. What would he say if I suggested it to him—that he come here? Worse, what would Mom say if she found out he was not only still hanging around, but had actually moved into town? Of course, he'd have to sell his condo and I'm not sure how willing he is to part with it, but the thought consumes me until I make it halfway around the garden.

There's a particularly fat dandelion clump trying to push its way into our lavender patch, with two round, shaggy flower heads poking up from the spiky leaves. A sudden impulse strikes and I reach out and yank both flower heads from their stems, then give them a good grind with the palm of my hand. They make a bright yellow smear on the concrete. I stare at them with satisfaction for a moment, then have to sit back on my heels and take a couple of breaths. For just a moment, those dandelion heads belonged to Gabe and Chance. I'm not given to violent outbursts—at least, I never have been before. But knowing how they made Asher feel last night has me more upset than I can ever remember being.

"Maybe they aren't who we thought they were," I mutter under my breath. I mean, after all, what kind of friends would accept a contract behind their bandmate's back and then lie about it?

An hour later, after the weeding, comes a cool shower and then lunch. I pick at my hastily made food and stare at my phone while sitting at the kitchen island, wondering why Asher hasn't called or even texted since last night. Maybe he's still sleeping? It was late, after all. There aren't even read receipts on the messages I sent him when I woke up.

I force myself to put the phone down and think about something else—anything else. But barely a second later there is a loud buzzing noise and I practically drop half my sandwich in my hurry to check the text. My heart is thumping hard and fast, but it sinks almost as quickly when I see who the message is from. It's a contact that isn't saved in my phone, but I remember the number because I've seen it pop up on my home screen a million times in the past.

EVAN: *Hey...can we talk?*

I swipe the notification away. The last person in the world I want to talk to right now is Evan. Another notification pops up to replace it almost immediately.

EVAN: *I miss you. I know what I did was wrong.*

Nothing comes in after that, so I finish my sandwich and rinse off my plate in the sink before turning around and staring at the empty house around me. What should I do now? Mom is locked in her room on the phone, probably talking to her best friend, Poppy, and complaining about Will while nursing her rodeo saddle sores. I don't feel like going anywhere, especially not after getting those texts. Why is Evan even texting me at all? It's not as if the conversation we had at the Buskers Festival actually went well. It might also be weird because I'm so used to thinking of him as reliable; texting one girl that he misses her while he's dating someone else just wasn't something I thought he would do. Was this what his texts to Livi were like before everything blew up in my face?

My neck feels tingly, like it's being irritated by a lizard or an errant shirt tag, and the sick feeling is back in my gut. I need to find something productive to do, something to take my mind off everything that's been going on, all the questions I have about why I'm getting texts from Evan but not Asher. But thinking about both of them in the same moment sends my mind spinning in another direction again.

Why hasn't Asher called or texted?

Has he changed his mind and tried to make up with the band?

What if that argument last night changed his mind about me? There are other girls he's told me about at the Festival, and I know that one in particular named Storm has been getting pretty friendly with the guys. I didn't see her the one night that I was there, but it makes me feel a little worried that perhaps Asher decided to go out with Gabe and Chance after all to a party, even though he's mad at them. It doesn't mean he's mad at every other performer—he could have avoided the guys and just went to see someone else.

I sigh, looking at the living room windows and the piano overlooking the garden I just cleaned up. There's nothing much left for me to do but practice, so I cross the room and take a seat on the bench. I lift the lid and place my hands on the keys. Like I always do before I play, I close my eyes and think for a moment, trying to visualize the music going through my head and out into my fingers. I remember the moment Asher and I wrote the end to "Mermaid Avenue," and the lyrics he sang to me last night for a new song that I accidentally spurred. As soon as I start thinking about Asher, the music begins to flow, and I lose myself.

I don't know how much time passes before Mom comes in and sits on the couch, right in the spot where Asher played his guitar one of the first nights here. I have my eyes closed so I don't see her, but I hear the squeaking of the cushions and when I'm done with my melody, I pause and look over.

"Shae, I've been thinking about what I said the other night. I should have trusted you more before I left. You're leaving in a few weeks for college and you're going to make your own, adult decisions. I need to respect that they're going to be good ones because you've learned well growing up."

I nod. "Thanks, Mom."

She gives me a little smile, tilting her head to the side like she's listening to music that isn't being played any more. "And that boy—Asher—I can tell he means something to you. Something important. I just want to make sure you're being careful. It's my job to worry, you know, as a mother. That's what we do."

"I am careful. I promise."

"I trust you, Shaeline."

Right at that moment my phone starts to buzz again, but the tone is more consistent, telling me a call is coming through. I flick my gaze up to Mom and then back to the phone and up to Mom again, silently asking for her permission to cut our conversation short and see who is on the line. The moment she bobs her head and goes to stand up and leave the room, I reach for the device and see Asher's name emblazoned on the screen. I wait for Mom to disappear into the kitchen before I press the green "call accept" button and watch his name blink twice.

"Hi!" My voice is overexcited, and I immediately try to dial down my relief. "I figured you must have been sleeping."

"I was. And I was thinking. You know, about what you said last night about how I should still go play this show because the audience won't know that it could be the last time Collide performs live. I'm going to play. I'm going to play the hell out of that show."

My phone buzzes again in my hand, and when I pull it away from my ear to check who is texting, I see another note from Evan.

> EVAN: *Shae, we really need to talk about us. Can you text me back? I'm sorry about making up all that stuff on the video...*

I swipe the message away again. I knew I should have blocked his number instead of just deleting it.

"Shae?" Asher says my name like it's a question. "Are you still there?"

"Yeah, I'm here. And I think you're making the right choice. It might be hard to show up there tonight, but I think you'd regret it more if you didn't go."

"I know. You're right. Listen, I just wanted to call you quick to let you know I'd decided to play. I wish you could be here to see it. I'd have loved to play my last show with you in the audience."

"Me too."

Silence encompasses us then, but not the awkward kind of silence that existed when Evan and Livi told me they were together while we met up at Barracuda's. It's more of a quiet contemplation, where we're both thinking something and not saying it. That is, until we do.

"I miss you," I say, whispering the words so Mom doesn't overhear.

"I miss you too. I'll talk to you after the show."

Asher and I say our goodbyes. I close the lid to the piano and am just about to escape up to my room when Mom sticks her head out from the kitchen while popping blueberries in her mouth.

"Not so fast, Shaeline."

I turn around slow, hoping that perhaps I'm hearing things. But it doesn't take her more than another second to give me a look that says I'm not about to like what comes next.

"You're not getting away that easily from your chores. I said I was going to try to trust you, but you still lied to me. There are three baskets of laundry that need to be done, and one in the dryer to fold and put away, plus whatever's in your room that I'm sure you haven't washed since I left."

Stifling a groan, I shove my phone in the back pocket of my shorts. There's a laundry pile as big as me hiding in my closet, along with what I brought home from Tampa still in my suitcase. "Sure, Mom. I'll start on it now."

Before she can give me anything else to do, I speed down the hall and disappear into the laundry room with my phone volume up, just in case Asher decides to text.

A couple of hours later, the mountains of laundry have diminished into small hills. I'm on the final load of towels from the main bathroom when I feel buzzing coming from my pocket, along with the trill of my ringtone. I pull the device out and stare down at the screen to another unmarked but familiar number, and I let the song play for a long while before I finally punch the button to answer the call, already knowing who is on the other end.

"Hello?"

"Shae, it's Livi."

My chest feels like it's clamped in a vice. "I don't want to talk to you."

"I know, I know, I'm sorry, but...but I didn't know who else to call." There's a shaky quality to her voice that doesn't sound at all like her. "I messed something up and then Evan got mad and left with the car, and now I'm stuck in Tampa and can't get home."

No wonder Evan has been harassing me all afternoon. It's terrible, but I can't bring myself to feel sorry; whatever they're fighting about, it is only their own fault. "So, call your mom or get a cab or something."

"I can't. Mom and Dad are at a charity event and don't know I'm in Tampa at all. They think I'm hanging out at Lyndsay's neighbor's house helping her watch their dogs while they're out of town. And I can't get a cab because my purse was in Evan's car and he won't answer my calls." She pauses here and I can hear her breath, heavy and distressed, on the other end of the line. "You're the only person I have left."

That isn't true and we both know it. She could call Lyndsay or Emily or one of our other friends. But she didn't...she called me. The person who was her best friend right up until the moment she chose to betray me. Silence hangs between us as we both wait to see who will break it first, stretching longer and longer. Then I hear the tiniest little squeak of a sob, and my lungs relax. Livi *never* cries.

"Where are you?"

The line crackles with her sigh of relief. "At Presto Pasta, across from The Park Royal."

I can't help but think that if I go to Tampa to pick up Livi, I might be able to see Asher. I could surprise him by being there in the crowd to watch the final Collide show. And plus, now that I'm on Mom's good side for doing chores all day, it shouldn't be a problem to get the car—especially to help Livi.

"It'll take me a bit to get there."

"I know. I just... Thank you."

I think about telling her that she owes me one, but instead, I just hang up.

Chapter Eighteen

ASHER

Every time I talk to Shae from the distance between Tampa and Emerald Beach, it makes me realize how much I miss her. But today, on top of missing her, it strikes me that I also need to have a conversation with Gabe and Chance to sort out what we're going to be doing for the rest of the summer. If they're signing with Black Horse and putting out an album, I can't imagine they're going to want to continue touring around Florida at these little festivals, though maybe they'll want the publicity. I'd probably just get in the way, but the more I think about it, the more I want to be in the way. I wrote songs for them for the better part of a year, and even though we worked on a lot of things together, I always thought it would be the three of us making music for a long, long time.

But now, my dream of spending however many future summers performing with my best friends has been smashed into a thousand little pieces—all thanks to one stupid contract.

Prodding the button on the side of my phone, I check for the time twice before it actually registers. Gabe and

Chance are probably still rehearsing for the show tonight, and if I leave now, I might be able to talk with them both about what's going on in my head. I mean, does the manager of Black Horse even know that I'm the main songwriter in the group, or does he not even care?

I grab my guitar case from the floor next to my bed and slip on a pair of sneakers before heading out of the condo. As I ride down the elevator, my heart starts racing; I'm thinking of all the things I could want to say to the guys to tell them exactly how betrayed I feel. By the time the door dings to let me know I've made it to the garage, there's heat in my cheeks and I'm nearly crushing the fabric case strap in my grasp. The sensation doesn't go away the entire drive across Genesis Lake toward the city. I think it gets worse the closer I get to Gabe and Chance's because as I pull into the visitor's lot of their apartment, I've clenched the steering wheel so tight my knuckles are white.

It takes me a minute or two to calm down, doing breathing exercises I remember hearing about on one of Mom's meditation class recordings. However, as soon as I slam the car door, the boiling in my stomach starts back up again. I immediately decide to leave my guitar behind because I know I won't be practicing with the guys today, and I walk up the pathway to the small, stucco building before punching the unit number into the keypad. It rings a couple of times before Gabe's voice comes over the speaker, his picture on the video screen above the doorbell. I shift my weight from one foot to another, a little lost for what I'm going to say. Despite having planned on giving them a piece of my mind, I'm drawing a blank.

Thankfully, Gabe speaks first. "Asher?"

He doesn't even bother to say hello, probably because he's just as surprised to see me as I am to even be here. Who knew a friendship could fall apart so quickly?

"Hey. Listen, can we talk?" I choke out the words, trying to sound confident when, in reality, it feels like Gabe and Chance hold all the cards.

Gabe's gaze flickers off the screen and I know he's looking at Chance for some guidance as to whether they're even going to let me into the apartment I was so welcome in only a few days before.

"Yeah. Come on up."

The video screen flickers off as the door buzzes, giving me about a three-second window to let myself in the complex. I rush through the atrium and down the first-floor hallway on the left, all the way to the end of the corridor where Gabe and Chance live. With every step my sneakers take, my heart must beat ten times, and the back of my neck starts to sweat, either from the Florida heat or my nerves finally getting the best of me.

I raise my hand to knock on the door, but it opens before I even have the opportunity.

"Hi." Gabe steps back from the entryway, letting me take an awkward step in, onto the tile floor. There's a familiar crack on one of the squares where we dropped an amplifier a few months back, and something crosses my mind to tell me that this might be the last time I ever see it.

"Hey, um… I guess I just wanted to figure out what the plan was for the rest of the summer with all our other contracts." I close the door behind me, and for a moment it feels as if the whole apartment is stifling hot. There's the faint smell of macaroni and cheese from the kitchen, and Chance is nowhere to be found. I suspect he's probably hiding in his bedroom, not one for conflict, leaving Gabe to do all the dirty work. I just never thought I'd be the one he was hiding from.

Gabe nods. "Yeah. I guess maybe we should talk about that."

We walk into the living room, instruments strewn about, while the coffee table is topped with pages upon pages of scratched-out words—lyrics. He pushes the sheets out of the way, shoving them underneath a notebook and some official-looking typed documents, and takes a seat in the ancient Papasan chair. I perch on the arm of the couch because the rest of the places to sit are covered in wrappers, music sheets, or instruments.

"So, I mean, I wasn't really sure—" I try to get my thoughts out, but Gabe interrupts me, leaning forward to adjust a chewed-up pencil that's about to roll off the tabletop.

"Listen, Asher, I know you usually write the songs and stuff like that, but Black Horse said they're going to get us writers and we'll do a little on our own. And with Chance able to play the guitar, it's just a smart business decision. Why would we want to split up the money with an extra person, if that extra person isn't really—"

"Isn't really what?" I wrinkle my eyebrows together. A strange pause sits between us, and I know immediately that this conversation is going downhill very quickly.

"They just—they said that it wasn't necessary. I mean, obviously Chance and I think you're necessary, but Black Horse didn't see it that way. And if we pushed them too much, we might not have even gotten the contract at all.

At least, the lawyer we saw thanks to Dad said that it could be something they'd do. Pull the offer back if we got too difficult."

I run a hand over my face, scrubbing at the little prickling stubble on my jaw. "I'm not sure how asking them to include all the members of the band is being too difficult."

Gabe leans back in the chair. "I don't know what you want me to tell you, Asher. This was our dream. Is our dream. If you were in the same position, what would you do? I mean, you spent our vacation with Shae, you brought her along to Tampa. Things are serious between you two, I can feel it. Chance knows too. It was only a matter of time before you left for something else anyway."

For a moment, I don't have any words. I hadn't ever thought of leaving Collide because of meeting Shae, but maybe the guys saw something that I hadn't even considered. I mean, after all, my level of involvement in relationships has been minimal at best. Adjusting my perch on the sofa arm, I bite at the inside of my lip to keep myself from saying something that I don't really want to. Or maybe I do—maybe I really want to tell Gabe where he and Chance can go. Maybe I want to tell him that I wouldn't have ever abandoned them like this, but when he words it the way he just did, I guess I'm not really sure what my choice would be.

"I never would have—"

Gabe sighs. "Yes, you would have, Asher. It's business, it's dreams, it's everything all rolled together. We've been working for this since we were kids. But you have more than we do. You have Shae, you have your music, and you have songwriting. The two of you can—I don't know. Maybe you can do something indie. Maybe her school will have a program. You've got options, you know. This, for Chance and me, this is our option."

It's my turn to exhale now, because I came here expecting to get mad and make a point, and all I'm getting is defeated and tired. "The rest of the summer?"

"Our manager's handling it."

I think for anyone else, their first thought would be to worry about money. These summer festivals were my way of making a living until mid-autumn when I'd have to find something else or do shows in the evenings or convince bar owners to let me play even though I'm barely underage. However, in this case, my first thought is about Shae. I can spend the summer with her. I can go back to Emerald Beach and, I don't know, work at Beaches N' Cream or Barracuda's until I'm able to figure out my next step. Or maybe she can come with me, come to Genesis Lake. A million ideas roll around inside me until I must appear so vacant that Gabe has to make a comment.

"Asher, I hate to kick you out or whatnot, but Chance and I really have to finish up what we're working on here."

"Yeah." I hoist myself up from the couch arm. "What about tonight?"

"Don't worry about it. We've got the rest of the Buskers Festival handled."

"Sure. Well, that's good then. I guess I'll just—I'll see you around."

There's quiet between Gabe and me, and when I head to the front door, I spot Chance's head peeking around the corner, casually trying to make it look like he hasn't been listening in on the conversation. I don't bother acknowledging him because it doesn't feel like there's a point anymore.

Gabe opens the door, the hallway drenched in sunlight from the large windows along one side of the corridor. "See you around."

I nod goodbye to that familiar cracked tile on the floor before stepping out of the apartment for what could very well be the last time ever.

When I get back to the car, I don't exactly want to go home. I check the time and it's only about an hour and a bit until the Buskers Festival is due to start for the night, and with nothing else to do, I take the long way to Tampa.

I let the car go a little too fast around the turns, speed a bit too high on the straightaways, but I can't help the feeling of being alive, and the underlying sensation of being let go from the dream I thought I had. Maybe this is some kind of a blessing in disguise, not having to choose between Shae and touring for the rest of the summer, though I was looking forward to it for the second year in a row. My thoughts wander as the crystal blue of the water twinkles in the distance, and I know that somewhere over in Emerald Beach, Shae's looking at the same gulf and maybe thinking about me too.

The long way around Tampa takes less time than I remember, but when I finally park downtown there's hardly any time before the bands are likely to be setting up. I tap my fingers on the steering wheel, a frustrated feeling sitting hard as a rock in my stomach. Unraveling the emotion, getting lost in my thoughts, it strikes me that I'm at least partially upset because I had my final show taken from me. I didn't know that my last show would be the only one I'd perform for the rest of my life with Collide, and somehow, I feel like something special has been taken from me. Who knows when I'm going to get back up on a stage again?

And then, I have an idea.

Rushing out from the car, I pocket my keys before grabbing my guitar off the back seat. I've found a parking spot close to the stages, and I head on a mission down toward the performance area. Crowds are just starting to mill around, forming underneath the heat of the Florida night, women in flowered dresses and men in deck shoes all walking about waiting for the shows to start. As I approach the Brackley Soundstage, I half expect to see Gabe and Chance there setting up the rest of their equipment, but the space is empty, which is exactly what I was hoping for.

I set my guitar case on the edge of the stage, unzip the zipper, and strum a couple of quiet chords just to make sure the instrument is still in tune. It is.

Feigning confidence and feeling nervous for one of the first times since I started performing, I step onto the soundstage in the bright lights that are ready for a band that doesn't exist any longer. There's a wooden stool near the far side of the stage with a microphone, the setup different than what we used before. Gabe and Chance must have been here, which means I don't have much time.

"Hi, everyone. My name's Asher and I was a member of the band Collide, who you'll see perform here shortly." My voice wavers just a little, but I clear my throat because if I'm going to sing one final time here on the Brackley Soundstage, I'd better make it worth it. "Due to a turn of events, I'm no longer a part of the group, but I wanted to have the opportunity to share a song with you all to send me off."

People finally stop walking, gathering around the staging and seemingly listening to what I'm saying. From farther off in the distance, I spot Chance and Gabe running toward me, probably ready to tear me off the stage and rip me a new one for pulling a stunt like this. But I keep talking, and as I talk, I strum a little on my guitar, warming up my fingers and my mind to sing and play at the same time.

"So, this is one of my new favorite songs. I've never shared it with anyone, but I thought I'd share it with you all since this is a special night. Because, like I said, this is my final night of performance until who knows when. I'm leaving after this to find my new girlfriend and I'm spending the summer with her. Then I'll figure the rest out later."

I strum a few other notes, fingers trickling over the strings. I'm not as great a speaker as Gabe is, so I'd best get playing.

"Anyway, for your enjoyment, here's a little song I wrote called 'Mermaid Avenue.'"

Humming a few notes, I catch Gabe and Chance's gaze the very moment I start to play. They halt at the edge of the stage, knowing things have already gone too far to turn back. And so, I sing the song I wrote for Shae that she didn't even know about until the moment I fell in love with her.

> *I wake in the empty morning, the space next to me cold*
>
> *I'm barely awake and I'm chaos and uncontrolled*
>
> *The sunrise is lemonade; but life's nothing but a fray*
>
> *My heart's beating but it's distant and astray*

The ocean's in front of us with the sandy edge of white

I'm indigo and she's all the stars in the night

But she's there and she's barely breathing

I'm here and my heart is bleeding

And I push through the three-in-the-morning thoughts

And I push through all the three-in-the-morning thoughts

As we turn off

And we turn on

Around the corner of a little place

Called Mermaid Avenue

Chapter Nineteen

SHAE

Mom doesn't seem to mind the idea of giving me the car to rescue Livi, though of course there's hesitation in her voice when I tell her that the rescuing will be taking place in Tampa. I have to regale to her the story about seeing Livi and Evan at the Buskers Festival and how that whole thing happened, including the argument we had in public. She seems understanding, given the circumstances, and hands me over the keys once she seemingly decides that I must be telling the truth about where I'm going. Plus, I make a million promises to be home as early as possible, only going to pick up Livi and heading straight back home. I don't bother telling her that Asher's going to be playing tonight as well, because it's not like I'm going to take a big detour. His set's only a half-hour and what's a half-hour in the grand scheme of things?

The drive to Tampa takes longer than I remember, probably because I'm alone. I flick between stations on the radio trying to find the classical one I used to have saved on the presets before eventually I give up and turn the music off. I've always liked listening to the road noise while driving; something about it is calming while still reminding me to pay attention to what I'm doing. The darkness of the water glistens to my right, sparkling with the fading sun, and a little smile creeps over my face as I pass the exit for Genesis Lake just as my cell phone rings on the car dashboard.

The caller ID says "unknown number," and usually I wouldn't bother answering those, but I've been by myself in this car for pushing on two hours and perhaps this might break up the drive a little. I poke the call answer button on the steering wheel.

"Hello?"

"Shae?" Evan's familiar voice comes through the car speakers loud and clear, and I think about hanging up before he has a chance to speak again. "Don't hang up, please."

"I don't want to talk to you, Evan. I have absolutely nothing to say. You could have ruined my entire summer."

"I know, I'm sorry. It was stupid. I didn't want Mom to hate Livi right off the bat so when she found the video of us in Beaches N' Cream I told her it was you. It was easier for it to be you and to break up with you after. I didn't think she was going to take away your job. I just thought that maybe it would be a good way to end things. For real."

I sigh as loud as possible, hoping Evan can hear my exasperation over the sound of the car tires on the pavement. "Well, she did, and it certainly ended things. Anything else?"

"Well, yeah. There's lots of other things I'd like to say to you, Shae. But I'm worried I'm not allowed to say them."

"Hurry up and say them, Evan. You're lucky I'm stuck in the car by myself for another fifteen minutes or I'd have hung up on you already."

There's a long pause then, so long that I wonder if the call's gotten disconnected. But when I look over at the dashboard screen, the counter is counting up, telling me that Evan's still on the line.

"Evan?"

The sound of a voice clearing comes over the speaker, and then shaky words. "I'm still in love with you, Shae."

I choke on my own spit, nearly driving the car off onto the shoulder of the road.

"Excuse me?"

"I left Livi in Tampa, Shae. I came home for you. I knew that I'd done something wrong the moment she and I arrived in the city, and I wasn't sure how to fix it. Then I saw you with that other guy—whatever his name is—and it kind of cemented the whole thing for me. He's not right for you. I'm right for you and I'm here now and I know it."

There's no helping myself when I start to laugh, and it comes from deep in my stomach to the point I'm glad there aren't many other cars on the road because I'm probably swerving all over my lane. It takes me a minute to calm down, the chuckles still rolling around in my throat when I speak again, Evan silent on the end of the phone where I picture him sitting on his bed waiting for me to say something that isn't straight up laughter.

"You can't be serious right now." I take the off ramp toward Tampa, knowing I'm only a few minutes from res-cuing my ex-best friend who my ex-boyfriend just admit-ted he abandoned in town. "I know about you leaving Livi in Tampa. I'm on my way to go and pick her up. And no, you don't still love me, Evan. I don't think you really ever did. Asher, on the other hand, well, that's something different. Entirely. Don't call me. Don't think about me. After I take Livi home, trust me, I won't be spending any more headspace on you."

"Shae—"

I punch the end call button and the car descends into an almost-silence as I merge onto the road toward Presto Pasta and The Park Royal. They're both in the middle of the city, near to the waterfront, but before I make my way down toward the gulf, I pull the car off onto the parking lot for the Ultra Gas station and block Evan's number from my phone. There's something relieving about the action, knowing that he can't contact me anymore. Knowing that once he goes away to school or Europe or wherever he decides to visit next, I won't have to be any part of the conversation.

When I pull back onto the road, it takes me another ten minutes to get to the parking lot for The Park Royal. I text Livi and try to call her, but her phone just rings and rings before going to voicemail, so I leave the car in one of the guest parking spaces and walk across the busy street only to find her coming around the corner with two cups of ice cream in her hands. The rosy labels tell me they're from Pinkie's down on the waterfront near the Brackley Soundstage where Collide has their shows. Or had, until they broke up—as of tonight.

"Hi!" Livi's voice is bright but her eyes are red as if she's been crying, which I know she has. "I got us some sorbet since I know you like that best. They had peach and strawberry, so I got one of each. You can pick which one you want."

"I'll take the peach." My voice has a flat undertone. Sorbet isn't going to fix anything between Livi and me. She slept with my boyfriend and messed up my summer and was all around just a horrible friend. Even still, I take the yellowy-orange dessert from her manicured hand and we sit on a bench in front of Presto Pasta. "How'd you pay for this? I thought your purse was in Evan's car?"

"Oh, I used Pre-Pay on my phone. I have one of my cards saved. I was kind of surprised that Pinkie's was technologically advanced enough to take a phone payment, but here we are. With sorbet."

Nodding, I scoop a half a mouthful of cold sorbet into my mouth, the taste of peaches running over my tongue and down the back of my throat. It's the perfect thing to eat on a hot evening like this, but truly all I want is to get down to the waterfront and watch Asher's show. In the distance, there's the sound of music and crowds that likely belong to the Buskers Festival, and I know that down there on the stage he's probably getting ready to perform with Gabe and Chance and I'm not even there to watch.

We eat most of our sorbet in silence, watching people walk past and avoiding the inevitable discussion about what Livi meant when she mentioned over the phone that she messed up something with Evan. When we were friends and we would sit on Emerald Beach and watch tourists go past, we used to make up stories about their lives and what we thought brought them to Florida, how many pets they owned, all things of that sort. However, now, maybe she's doing that in her head because she certainly isn't doing it out loud. Me, on the other hand, I've completely drawn a blank to think about anything but what "I messed up" could possibly mean, from cheating on Evan with someone else, to finding out she's pregnant.

"So," I say as I dig out the final mouthful of my peach dessert. "Are you going to tell me what happened? You said that you messed up something when you called, and then Evan called me on the way here and told me that he left you."

Livi rolls her eyes as she drops her cup and spoon into the garbage can by her side of the bench. "Evan's so dramatic."

I want to remind her that she's the one who called me bawling, asking for me to come to Tampa to pick her up after she lied to her parents about where she was going, but I don't bother. I'm supposed to be the bigger person here, even though I did just block Evan from ever contacting me again.

"So, what happened then?" I pry her for more information, not able to help but wondering what time it is and if we are going to miss Asher's next set as well.

"Oh." She rubs at the corner of her eye, making the skin pink to accent the redness. "It's just stupid, really. We just argued over who was going to pay the hotel bill and check out is tomorrow, and I panicked a bit because my purse was gone, but you can totally get me, right?"

For a moment, I have no words because I'm both relieved and intensely angry. My heart smashes against my ribs and my hands start to shake on the little paper bowl of melted sorbet remnants. Livi really dragged me two hours away from Emerald Beach to come pick her up because she and Evan got in a fight over who was going to pay a bill for a hotel they weren't even supposed to be at? I can't believe it—or that I was so gullible to come to her rescue when really, she didn't need saving at all.

"You mean that you're not pregnant or cheating or—"

Livi chokes out a laugh, much like the one I gave Evan when he told me that he was still in love with me. "Oh God, Shae. No, nothing like that. Can you imagine if I was pregnant with Evan's baby? That's like, a big no."

Kind and understanding words fail me, and my mouth starts spewing words before my head can even think about what I'm saying.

"You really, *really* called me up after having videotaped sex in Beaches N' Cream with my boyfriend to come and get you two hours away, only to tell me that you argued with said boyfriend over who was going to pay a bill? Livi, you have to be the most selfish, ridiculous, self-centered, arrogant—"

I only pause for a second because Livi starts to cry, a big, fat, fake tear rolling over her pink cheeks. When she's truly upset, her bottom lip quivers. It's not moving this time, which tells me that the droplet on her skin is being forced out to try to make me feel bad for what I'm about to say. It doesn't work.

"I can't believe I was ever friends with you." I spit the words across the bench before rising to my feet and dumping my empty Pinkie's cup in the garbage can. "Don't you ever contact me again. Don't rely on me for anything. Call Evan this time and figure your shit out and get him to help you, because I'm not here anymore."

"Shae—"

"I'm done, Livi. Done with a capital D."

I turn on my heel and stomp past Presto Pasta and down around the corner toward the Brackley Soundstage, where I know deep in my heart I can hear Asher and Gabe and Chance playing something familiar over the noise of the crowds. Maybe it's all in my head, or because of the emotions I'm feeling over leaving Livi there on the corner in front of The Park Royal, but as soon as the salty ocean water scent hits my face when I come around the building, real tears start to stream down my face. I try to hide my eyes as I pass tourists and walkers, blindly marching across the road to the waterfront where I know I'll find Asher and be able to tell him in between sets that I've blocked Livi and Evan from my life for good.

Groups of people move out of my way as I cross to-ward the Buskers Festival, avoiding me like something's wrong. And maybe it is. Maybe I've truly lost my best friend. Or maybe she never really was a very good friend after all.

When I approach the Brackley Soundstage, there's a crowd already formed and a single, familiar silhouette sits on the stage playing a song I know all too well. I know it because I helped write the bridge to the final chorus, and that's when I realize that Asher's on the stage by himself, Gabe and Chance standing in the wings and the shadows, looking across at the boy playing the song I know he wrote for me.

> *We collide, the night barely awake, the moon alive in the dark*
>
> *Fingers twisted around one another*
>
> *Bodies like waves*
>
> *Hearts like sirens*
>
> *Souls entwined, we collide*

As I push through the crowd to stand near the front, my movement seems to catch Asher's eye because he looks up from his strumming and gives me the biggest smile. It's almost as if he knew I was going to show up, even without me having told him for certain that I would be here.

But she's there and she's barely breathing

I'm here and my heart is bleeding

And I push through the three-in-the-morning thoughts

And I push through all the three-in-the-morning thoughts

As we turn off

And we turn on

Around the corner of a little place

Called Mermaid Avenue

I sing along to the final words of the song under my breath, my lips hardly moving so the people in the groups at the front of the stage don't notice that I'm familiar with the music.

As we turn off

And we turn on

Around the corner of a little place

Called Mermaid Avenue.

As Asher gives a final hum to the melody, the crowd erupts into applause and my heart swells a million times because I know that Collide may be over, but Asher's music career is just beginning.

Chapter Twenty

ASHER

The second I spot Shae in the crowd it's as if all of a sudden everything seems to be okay. I know I belong up here and I'm not taking the spotlight away from Gabe and Chance or Collide or whatever it is they're going to be called now that they've signed to Black Horse Records without me. This is my spotlight, the one I own for this moment, and the crowd is cheering and applauding for me and my rendition of "Mermaid Avenue," a song I never thought I'd perform here in Tampa in front of anyone. It feels good. Like a piece of my soul has been put back together, knowing that I can make groups respond the way they are, even if it's just smacking their hands together and hopefully connecting with a few of the stanzas that I sang.

"Thanks so much, everyone. I really appreciate the opportunity to come here tonight and play for you. If you don't mind, the girl who inspired that last song is here now, and I'd like to call her up on stage and have her play one final song with me."

Beckoning to Shae who stands off to the edge of the steps near Gabe and Chance, I gesture toward the keyboard that's already set up to my right. I know I really shouldn't put her on the spot like this, especially since she's nervous about playing in public, but she did such a great job last time that I can't help myself. Thankfully, after only a second of hesitation, Shae steps onto the Brackley Soundstage, giving a shy little wave to the crowd before she approaches me and covers the microphone with her hand.

"Have you totally lost it?"

I smile, because there's nothing else left for me to do, sliding my fingers over the strings of the guitar and feeling their pressure. "I haven't lost anything. I've found something though. And I want to share it with everyone standing out there right now. I want to let Gabe and Chance and the world know that a summer—a person—can change everything."

Shae's mouth quirks up at the corner, her dark hair blowing around her cheeks in the breeze. "What were you thinking?"

"I want to play 'The Summer I Loved You.' I think it would be the perfect thing to leave Collide behind with. A new song that's ours that they'll never get."

Lifting her hand off the microphone carefully, Shae takes a deep breath and holds it for a second before she gives me a little nod of acceptance. She walks a few steps over with new confidence and pokes at the dials on the keyboard for a second to make sure everything's just so for the song. My heart is full, and I strum a note or two before I speak to the gathering of people that's grown since Shae came on stage. The spotlight's in my eyes but the silhouettes of the people on the waterfront are clear, and the crowd buzzes with what I can only assume is anticipation for what's going to happen next and the potential drama to follow.

"Can I get a round of applause for Shae? She's headed off to the University of Tampa to study piano this year, and I am so happy she's agreed to play this last song with me."

The crowd breaks into scattered clapping and Shae's face glows a hot pink at the attention, while Gabe and Chance stew in the background. When I hold up my hand, the applause stops, bodies shuffling to get the best view of the stage.

"We've titled this one 'The Summer I Loved You'—in memory of all the unexpected summers. The summer of surprises and feelings and firsts. The summer of the moments in between."

I pick away at a few notes before I swap my gaze over to Shae who has her hands poised on the keys of Gabe's keyboard, ready for the melody. Giving her what I hope is a reassuring grin, I play the first chord and she joins in right away with the gentle notes of the piano.

Surprise

I fell in love

For the first time

Maybe the last time

And surprise

It's not the way

I expected or

She expected but

Surprise

We tripped over all the

Moments that are in between

There are a few strums and a few beats until the chorus starts, and admittedly, I'm surprised when Shae's delicate singing voice comes in on the chorus line. The farther along in the lyrics we go, the stronger she gets, the wavering in her song changing to something emotional and calculated.

And I said hello

Hello to the summer I loved you

And goodbye

To the places I thought I'd never go

And surprise

To the feelings I never knew I'd ever keep

All because I said hello

Hello to the summer I loved you

We beam at each other for the moment in between the chorus and the next verse, which she leaves to me to sing alone.

Surprise

We stumbled

All over each other

And into the way we feel

And surprise

I never knew that

These things could happen

When you least expect them but

Surprise

We fell head over heels and

It's everything

Without even looking over at Shae, I know she's going to join in on the chorus. I can feel our connection through the song, strong as a wave and deep as the ocean. Though I do peek to see what she's doing, if she's okay, if she's feeling overwhelmed by the music or the stage or the crowd, what I spot is a girl who is totally in love with the way she can make the lyrics flow into a chorus.

And it's perfect. Everything about the moment is perfect, from the way Gabe runs his hand over his face to Chance practically stomping his foot as he knows he'll never write something that matches up to the sensation this song is giving Shae and me right now. From the crowd, waving and swaying in the Tampa summer air, to Shae's closed eyes, probably feeling every note she plays using the borrowed keyboard that she isn't even used to making music on.

And I said hello

Hello to the summer I loved you

And goodbye

To the places I thought I'd never go

And surprise

To the feelings I never knew I'd ever keep

All because I said hello

Hello to the summer I loved you

The song trickles off after that, Shae and I improvising an ending we never ended up writing because we ran out of time. It doesn't matter, though, because it's kind of like us. We haven't written an ending for us, either, and maybe we don't have to. Maybe we'll never have to. Because maybe we'll always have summer and Florida and music and each other.

I don't get an opportunity to thank the crowd for listening or enjoy the applause Shae and I get that rumbles over the waterfront and the Brackley Soundstage, because before we take up any more of the limelight, Gabe and Chance come running on the stage to shove us off the platform. Shae's giggling and smiling as she grabs my hand, nearly tripping over my soft guitar case as we are ushered away from the performance area and into the shadows of some manicured bushes.

"You've really lost it this time, Ash," Chance's voice is accusatory, like I've done something to him personally instead of the other way around. "You can't just crash our show like that."

"I'm sure you'll be able to make up for the five minutes of lost time. Plus, you're getting paid and I'm not, so think of it as money for time you didn't even have to work."

Chance steps forward with fury in his gaze like I've never seen before because he's usually one to avoid confrontation. That's the moment when I smell the beer on his breath and realize that both he and Gabe were out celebrating, probably with their new manager, right before they showed up here. We never drank before shows in the past, but I guess Collide isn't really Collide anymore, so maybe the rules have changed. The morals have changed. Everything, in some way, has changed.

"Come on, Ash." Shae tugs gently at my hand. "Let's just go."

I have so many things I want to say to my ex-best friends, words I didn't get out when I was talking to Gabe at their apartment. But Shae's touch grounds me and reminds me that none of it matters any more, because we're moving on without Collide, hopefully to something bigger and better.

Gabe and Chance recede into the spotlight, picking up from where we left off as I stuff my guitar back into the case and sling it over my shoulder.

"What are you doing here, anyway?" I ask, Shae leading the way off the boardwalk and up the waterfront sidewalks.

"I came to rescue Livi. She and Evan got into an—you know what? It doesn't matter. I don't think I'll be hearing from Evan or Livi ever again. I'm pretty sure I made my point when I saw her up at Presto Pasta, telling me that she dragged me all the way down here because of something stupid."

"Seems like both of our sets of friends aren't very good friends at all."

"I think people grow apart. It happens. That's what Mom told me happened to her and Dad. They were young when they met and then as they got older, they just became different people."

Nodding, we turn up one of the side streets toward the car park spaces near The Park Royal. "Sometimes people grow together, too, though."

Shae's tinkling laughter echoes over the distant sound of the crowd and mingles with the impending moonlight and stars. "Well, there's always that."

We walk along in silence for another minute or so before stopping next to the car I'm vaguely familiar with from her driveway on Mermaid Avenue.

"You heading back now? Or do you have some time to come to the condo?" My words are hopeful because I'd really like a few minutes alone with her right now, time to absorb everything that's happened tonight and put it in a place in my memory where I can access it for a long, long time.

She shakes her head. "I told Mom I'd pick up Livi and come right home. I'm already late as it is since I stopped to argue with her and then came to part of the show. I don't need another lecture about doing things I'm not supposed to while I'm under Mom's roof, even if it is only a few weeks until I move."

My heart sinks a little in my chest, disappointed that I won't have the chance to kiss her in private or have her listen to any of the number of melodies I've been working on since "The Summer I Loved You." But I can't help but understand. When Dad was alive, both my parents were the same way, trying to keep tabs on me for as long as possible. Then, Dad passed away and only six short years later, Mom knew she had to give up and let me be. Now she and I don't often know if we're even in the same state. It's like she let go all at once and never looked back from her freedom from me. I'm okay with it. I never grew attached to people much. At least, not until now.

"Maybe—" Shae pauses, her expression thoughtful. "Maybe you can come back to the Beach for a visit soon? I know it's not long until I'm in Tampa and we're closer, but I don't know if I can live without seeing you for that long. It feels like—"

"A lack of oxygen?"

She lets go of my hand and fishes out a car key from somewhere in her pocket, all while smiling. "Something like that. But I was thinking more in comparison to music. It's like together we're long, whole notes. But apart, we're rests, we're silent, we're breaks between the melodies just hoping for the notes to come together again in a loud crescendo."

I can't help myself then, because when Shae starts talking about music, it does something to my insides. Maybe it's the passion in her voice or the twitch in her lip or the way her eyes sparkle when she uses the term "crescendo," but I step in toward her. And as I step in toward her, I tip her chin toward me, and I look down toward her smile and the cherry-red of her lips.

"I'm so in love with you."

She doesn't have a chance to reply because I kiss her then, dipping in to press her against the passenger's side of the car while our mouths dance a melody of their own. I don't care about the people walking by the side street on the walkway, the sounds of footsteps and music as the soundtrack to our embrace. What I care about in the moment is her, the way she feels, and the sensation of her body touching mine while I remember that I am fully capable of falling for someone.

Shae kisses me back, hard, and the world melts away as it always does. Our fingers intertwine as the key for the car gets shoved back into her pocket, my other hand finding her hair and the back of her neck and settling onto the surface of the skin. By the time we separate it feels as if the sky has drawn darker, and the moon has risen higher, and we're one body in two pieces that move in unison, something that I'll probably be able to write into a song when I get back to the condo, alone.

"Are you sure you can't come back with me?"

Another small chuckle comes from deep in her throat as she brushes her hair back from her face and the breeze.

"I'm sure, Asher. But I'll call you when I get home, okay?"

I fight the urge to kiss her again, running every possible scenario in my head where I don't have to let her go back to Emerald Beach alone. "How about we compromise? We go back to the condo for ten minutes, I pack a bag, and I come back with you?"

Her eyes brighten immediately. "You can do that? Right now?"

"What else am I doing? It's not like I have a band anymore." I hoist the guitar up on my shoulder again before it slips down my arm and crashes against the sidewalk. "I'll find a hotel or something to stay at and it will be fine, I can hang out for a few days, we can figure things out, drink some Frozen Rockets, walk on the beach..."

"No hotel." Shae's practically bouncing with excitement. "You'll stay at the house. Mom will probably put you up in the guest room across the hall but that doesn't mean you can't sneak over once she's gone to bed. I'm sure she won't mind. It'll be fine. I just know it will. I'll call her before I head to the condo and let her know the plan."

"If not, there's the place Gabe and Chance and I stayed at that's not too far. We'll work it out."

Shae pokes the key fob to unlock the car doors and pulls her phone from her back shorts pocket. "Okay. I'll see you in a little bit then? I'll phone Mom now."

Giving her a quick kiss on the forehead, I run my hand down her bare arm before we part. She smells like sunshine and tastes like peach sorbet and feels like the best summer I've ever had. It's at that moment a new song starts to play in my head, something with just the piano and the guitar and our voices singing, performing the lyrics in wherever we decide to go next. In my head it's a bar in the dark, with exposed brick walls and fairy light jars on the tables. In her head—well, it could be a concert hall with a thousand people. But it doesn't matter. Because we're both concert halls and fairy lights and packed auditoriums and small spaces rolled together in one.

And when we are together, we are invincible.

Acknowledgements

Writing a book can be an isolated experience. There are hours spent behind a keyboard plotting and planning, typing and thinking. However, none of my stories have been put together in complete solitude, for which I am eternally grateful.

There are two people who particularly influenced the creation of *The Summer I Loved You*, offering guidance, care, and compassion.

To my husband, Jesse, who continually encourages my writing and imagination. I value all of your patience, kindness, and support for every one of my stories. You are the reason I'm able to write books, and spend nights in my office diving into the worlds I've created in my head. I both love and appreciate you.

To my wonderful critique partner and friend, Britain Kalai Soderquist. From reading early drafts to providing feedback to make Shae and Asher's story engaging, you were absolutely as important to completing this story as I was.

Thank you both from the bottom of my heart.

And, finally, thank you to every reader for picking up this book. I truly hope you enjoy reading about Shae and Asher's journey.

About Nicole Bea

Nicole Bea is a technical writer and author who focuses on deep stories to dig into: books that include romance, honesty, hope, and self-discovery. An avid storyteller since childhood, she has honed her skills through a variety of educational programs including management, sociology, legal studies, and cultural diversity in the workplace, most recently engaging in coursework about communication for technologists. She loves books of all shapes and sizes, but has a soft spot for short reads, protagonists with pets, and anything featuring ghosts or cats.

When Nicole isn't busy updating her manuscript portfolio or catching up on her To Be Read pile, she can usually be found gardening, horseback riding, or perusing the shelves of a used bookstore. She and her husband share their home in Eastern Canada with a collection of multi-colored cats and a lifetime's worth of books.

Facebook
www.facebook.com/nicolebeawrites

Twitter
@nicolebeawrites

Website
www.nicolebea.com

Instagram
www.instagram.com/nicolebeawrites

Also from NineStar Press

Breaking the Ice by K.R. Collins

Sophie Fournier is the first woman drafted into the North American Hockey League. Playing hockey is something she's done all her life, but she faces new challenges as she finds her place on the struggling Concord Condors. She has to prove herself better than her rival-turned-teammate, Michael Hayes, and her rival-turned-friend, Dmitri Ivanov, and she has to do it all with a smile.

If she's successful then she opens the door to other women being drafted. She can't afford to think about what happens if she fails. All she knows is this: if she's not the best then she doesn't get to play.

No pressure, though.

Border CTRL + ESC by Ivy L. James

In the United States...

Mariana Mitogo is struggling to make ends meet. Then, out of the blue, she learns she's to receive a huge inheritance that would erase all her debt. The problem: she has to be married for six months to receive it, and her dating life is nonexistent.

In Spain...

Santiago de los Reyes, Mariana's Internet friend, has drained his bank account to support his family. Desperate to get his mom the heart surgery she needs, he interviews for a better-paying job that would take him from Madrid to Virginia. When he's offered the position but can't get a work visa, Mariana offers a solution that benefits both of them—a fiancé visa and a quick wedding.

If anyone finds out it's a green-card marriage, Santiago will be deported. Mariana would face a colossal fine and jail time. Good thing they're committed actors.

But as Santiago and Mariana pretend to build a life together, the lines blur between charade and reality. Will they dare to choose the love that feels more honest every day?

Connect with NineStar Press

www.ninestarpress.com

www.facebook.com/ninestarpress

www.facebook.com/groups/NineStarNiche

www.twitter.com/ninestarpress

www.instagram.com/ninestarpress